KAYLA WREN

Autumn Tricksters

BLACK CHERRY
PUBLISHING

First published by Black Cherry Publishing 2020

This novel is entirely a work of fiction. The names, characters and incidents portrayed in it are the work of the author's imagination. Any resemblance to actual persons, living or dead, events or localities is entirely coincidental.

Kayla Wren asserts the moral right to be identified as the author of this work.

First edition

ISBN: 978-1-8381116-2-5

Cover art by JS Designs

This book was professionally typeset on Reedsy.
Find out more at reedsy.com

Contents

Chapter 1

I step one foot back in the carnival and thank God I'm home. Three weeks in Ohio with my straight-laced family was a nightmare. I haven't breathed right since I left this place, since I heard the shriek of the crowd, the roar of flames, the pounding of drums. The scent of popcorn and roasting nuts floats to me on the breeze, and my stomach rumbles.

Finally. It's been three weeks too long.

I nod to the men and women running the stalls. There are shooting games, with the *plink* of air rifle pellets and the clatter of cans dropping to the ground. There are drinks stalls, with fresh roasting coffee and beer on tap. There are tents with fortune tellers; mimes with painted faces, striding through the crowd on stilts; pink vats of cotton candy.

It's a wonderland. An eerie, feral wonderland, where you're just as likely to have your pocket picked as your fortune told.

No sticky fingers come near my pockets. I'm one of these people, and they know better than to go for their own.

I hitch my duffel bag up on my shoulder and weave my way across the carnival grounds. The drink is flowing tonight; the townies getting messy and loud. They shove each other and cackle, their inhibitions slipping away in the carnival's haze. I skip around them, no one coming within an inch of my skin.

Sure, I could stamp my steel-toed boots and barge my way through. But I've had an eight-hour journey with a caffeine headache and a throbbing wrist. I know when to pick my battles. So I duck and weave my way through the crowd, like they're rocks and I'm water flowing around them.

"Hazel!" An older woman running one of the food stalls yells and waves her entire arm. I grin and cut over to her, sniffing at the hot dogs grilling on her cart.

"Hey, Ginny."

I drop my duffel at the base of her stand. Two soft, plump arms wrap around me and pull me close, and I pat her back awkwardly with my cast. When I pull away, one of her long grey hairs sticks to my tongue. I spit it out, grimacing at her roar of laughter.

"You've been away too long, girl."

"Tell me about it."

If I'd had my way, I'd never have left at all. Not even after everything that happened. This is my home.

"Robbie gave you the green light to come back?"

I shrug. "Something like that."

Ginny slices a bun as she talks, her hand deft with the knife. Ginny may look like a sweet old grandma, with her salt and pepper hair and flowery smock dresses, but she can gut a troublemaker quicker than a fish.

The truth is, I never asked for permission to come back. I should never have let them send me away in the first place. If I hadn't been so messed up—freaking out over my busted wrist, heart cracked open by my asshole ex—I'd have stood my ground. Insisted on staying here and resting up in my trailer.

Being home did nothing for me. I didn't get to laze around and eat my Mom's treats, or whatever Robbie expected. I got lectures and disappointed sighs. Pointed looks at my tattoos, my purple hair. A couple of nights, a bible was left pointedly on my bedside table. I came away with raised blood pressure and my fill of fucking cornfields.

Yeah. That was no healing retreat. If Robbie wants to send me away to lick my wounds, next time he can shell out for a spa.

Ginny pushes a steaming hot dog into my good hand, loaded up with crispy fried onions. I groan and snatch up the mustard and ketchup, lashing them on top.

"You're a goddess. A fucking deity." I take a bite and my eyes practically cross.

Ginny laughs and slaps me hard on the back, hard enough that greasy onions shower onto my boots.

"Get gone before Robbie sees you. I ain't wading into that."

It's more than fair, so I balance my hot dog on my cast and swing my duffel back onto my shoulder. Robbie will ream me out when he sees I'm here, and there's no call to drag Ginny into that. Robbie may be young, may be quiet and watchful, but he runs this whole show. When he says jump, we ask how high.

Apart from me, I guess. Just this one time.

I take another bite of my hot dog, burning the roof of my mouth, and plunge back into the mass of people. I tap the toe of my boots on the grass as I walk, dislodging the onions. It's dark, the air nipped with autumn cold, and the flames of the fire eaters burst in glowing pillars over the heads of the crowd.

I take one look at those flames and change course.

I'm not in the mood for Kamran Lajani.

Frantic drums sound from the big top tent on the edge of the carnival. I stare at it for a moment, almost sick with longing.

3

Lit up against the night sky, it looms over the grounds, calling to us and watching over us like our own temple. It's striped midnight blue and lilac, a creature of the night like us, blending in with the shadowed mountain peaks all around.

I should be in there right now; I should be on that trapeze. Soaring weightless over the crowd, twisting and swinging, buoyed by their gasps. Chalk coating my palms and crammed under my nails. Sweat slicking my skin.

I grunt and tuck my cast to my chest, shoving the last of the hot dog in my mouth.

Soon. Then I'll show these townies what's up.

I hate to go in there when I can't perform, but I head for the gaping mouth of the big top. Robbie keeps a watchful eye over the whole carnival, but he's especially careful with the circus acts. The performers put their lives on the line with every single performance. There are no safety nets and hidden lines here. We do this for real.

Even though it's his damn circus, Robbie fucking hates the risks. When Yan dropped me three weeks ago—dropped me in all the possible ways—I became a prime example of the perils of aerial work.

Robbie won't be happy to see me back so soon. Well, tough shit.

I veer away from the bustling main entrance, around the side of the tent. There's always a slit or two in the canvas, left behind by roadies so they can haul equipment in and out. Finding a gap in the heavy cloth, I duck inside, moist heat washing over me like I'm stepping into a greenhouse. My duffel catches on the flap as I move deeper inside and I lurch, instinctively flexing my hand in my cast. Burning pain lashes through my wrist, and I blink away the tears brimming in my eyes.

4

Damn tent.

Damn wrist.

Damn piece-of-shit duffel.

I clear my throat and straighten my shoulders, though no one can see me here in the shadows. Keeping to the edge of the crowds, I circle around the big top interior.

Robbie is exactly where I knew he'd be. He stands with his boots planted and his arms crossed, eyes glued on the performer spinning overhead. I glance up, following his line of sight—it's Aleksi, our headliner. The face on all our posters—and what a face. I used to love watching him work, gasping at the fluid way he spun on the silks like a spider weaving a web.

But Aleksi is the spitting image of his brother Yan, and the sight of him now makes the hot dog lurch in my stomach.

Doesn't matter. I duck my head and make a beeline for the man in charge. If any visitors were to glance at Robbie, they'd probably think he was a roadie. He's young: early thirties with sandy blond hair and scruff on his chin. He dresses all in faded black—thick work pants and a long-sleeved t-shirt. A tool belt hangs around his hips, and a radio crackles on the belt.

He looks unimportant. A small cog in a vast machine.

First rule of the carnival: appearances can be deceiving. He's not just some roadie. Robbie's our puppet master.

"Hey, boss." I give him my most winning smile as I plant myself square in front of him. Better not to dance around the point—I came back uninvited.

Robbie's eyes flick down, and irritation ripples across his face. He lowers his chin to stare me down, jaw clenching.

"Did I say you could come back?"

His Scottish accent always makes him sound softer than he

really is.

"Probably not," I say cheerfully, dropping my duffel at his feet. "But I got this sixth sense. Figured you missed me."

"You figured wrong." Robbie nudges my bag with his boot, nose wrinkling like I've brought him a dead mouse. "You messed yourself up. You can't work like that, Hazel."

He means my busted wrist; the bones still throbbing in my cast. I know he's right, that there's no reason for him to house and feed me while I can't even perform, but there is no way on this planet I'm about to turn tail and slink off back to the cornfields.

"I'll work a stand. Hook-a-Duck or some shit." I force another smile, trying not to let the hurt reach my face. I know Robbie's my boss and he doesn't owe me shit, but it's cold for him to dismiss me like that. Like I hurt myself because I was careless, not like a cheating scumbag literally dropped me.

Like this isn't my home just as much as his.

Come on, man, I urge him in my brain. *Muster up an emotion.*

Robbie looks at me, face as blank as a marble statue, then slides his gaze back up to Aleksi.

"Fine," he mutters, not even looking at me anymore. "But you'll earn your keep, same as everyone else."

Asshole. I never said I wouldn't, and I resent the implication. But I keep my face carefully blank to match his, leaning down to scoop up my duffel.

"Always a pleasure, boss man."

Robbie rolls his eyes without even looking down.

* * *

There's a random girl in my trailer.

My cold, dead little heart sings as I near the battered hunk of metal, its surface littered with dents and scratches. It's older than me, this piece of junk, but it's the truest home I've ever had. I've had three years to make it my own, from the fairy lights strung up inside to the mint plants lining the windowsill.

I stomp up the squeaking steps and barge the door open with my hip, only to find a pair of eyes blinking from my bed.

"What?" I crane my head back out the doorway, thinking I've gone wrong. That exhaustion got the better of me, and I've wandered up to the wrong trailer. But no—this is definitely mine. Right next to the door is the lucky number thirteen I screwed onto the side.

"Um," the girl says. "Who are you?"

Fuck this. I leave for three weeks and they reassign my trailer? After over three damn years of working here?

Did Robbie not think I was coming back at all? If I hadn't just shown up like this, would he ever have called me back? Hurt and panic squirm in my chest, and I tamp them down.

"Hazel. This is my trailer. Who the fuck are you?"

"Danika." The girl frowns like I'm the unreasonable one. I'm not curled up on someone else's bed. I hand-stitched that damn quilt, for fuck's sake! You could DNA-test me by the blood spatters.

I stomp over, dropping my bag on the mattress.

"All right, Danika, look alive. You're not staying here. This is the quilt I made last year. Those are the books I bought in the last town's flea market. That is my goddamn shampoo, which you better not have been using, by the way."

The girl watches my finger jabbing at various items in the trailer, her short curly brown hair bobbing as her head moves. She swallows hard, but when she looks back at me, resentment

7

burns in her eyes.

"Maybe you should have packed better when you left."

Oh, ho. No. I can't have that. If I let that kind of disrespect stand, the other carnies will walk all over me. I grab her by the ear, pulling her off the bed and marching her to the other end of the trailer. There's a second bed, one I used to use as a reading nook. I shouldn't even have to share that much—only first timers and kids don't get their own trailers.

But what can I say? I guess I'm in a generous mood.

Or maybe I don't want to test Robbie's patience again so soon.

"You can sleep here." I shove the girl down on the bed and push my hair back from my face. It's sweaty work, rearranging a trailer. "Touch my stuff again and you'll lose a finger. Tomorrow we'll get Robbie to give you your own place."

The look she shoots me is pure venom, but she doesn't fight back. She clambers fully onto the mattress, resting her back against the wall, and glowers at me as I make a heap of her stuff.

"This will go faster if you help." I wave my cast at her and she lets out a huff.

"Didn't want to lose a finger," she grumbles, but she slides off the mattress and comes over. I grin, elbowing her in the ribs as she gathers up an armful of her stuff.

"Cheer up, D. It could be worse. I could want to live with you."

Her eyes close and she shudders at the thought.

Yeah. The feeling's mutual.

Chapter 2

We pack up and leave the next day. There's some townie drama—a fight last night that got out of hand. Apparently one guy smashed his beer bottle on a stall and stuck it in his buddy's gut. It'll be about one of three things: a girl, a debt, or a sports team.

No way is Robbie sticking around to untangle that mess. We're pulling up tent pegs and packing trucks before the sun's broken over the horizon.

I stifle a yawn behind my cast as I help pack up boxes. I'm pretty useless without two working hands, but I'm pitching in the best I can. The worst thing someone can say about you at the carnival is that you're lazy.

I pull my weight, whatever Robbie implied. I always have.

Danika stomps past, a canvas bag stuffed with tent canvas weighing down her shoulder. Those things weigh a ton—usually it takes two men to slug those around. My new roomie may be thin as a rod, but apparently she's strong as one too. My mouth quirks into a smile at her back, though she can't see it.

"Playing nice, then?"

Robbie stops at my side, eyes roving over my work so far. He can inspect all he likes; I'm working fast and hard, same as everyone else. Even with a bum wrist, I know how to pack a truck.

"Not nice enough to keep sharing."

Bitterness is thick in my voice, but I force a playful smile to my lips.

I don't fool Robbie. I never do.

"I wasn't asking."

He pulls a pack of cigarettes out of his back pocket and taps them on his palm. He quit smoking two seasons ago, but he still carries the pack around like a security blanket. He fiddles with that packet a lot when I'm around. I think I mess with his blood pressure.

I guess I can't judge. Yan's locket still hangs around my neck, even after he stomped on my heart and got me benched in one horrible night. It's dumb, but I've worn it every day for so long I feel naked without it.

"None of the other headliners have to share." I swallow hard, trying to keep my voice even. "You're punishing me, Robbie. For getting hurt."

He hums, like he's heard my idea and he's considering whether it has merit.

"You're not a headliner right now, Hazel. You shouldn't even be back yet. So you'll be sharing a trailer, same as the other stand workers." His blue eyes flick to mine. "No special treatment."

The idea that Robbie would ever treat me as more than a tool on his belt is laughable. I'm an asset when I'm working, and I'm a nuisance now I'm not.

"Got it."

I may have to follow his orders, but I won't pretend to like them. I keep my head down and pack up the cooking

10

equipment, ignoring him outright. It's risky, bordering on disrespect, but I can't keep my temper in check right now. My shoulders finally relax when he sighs and walks away.

Good. Robbie flusters me, and I don't need that shit right now. I already made nice with one guy, and look where that got me. Popping painkillers and sharing my trailer, trying not to sniffle too loud at night when I let myself be pathetic for exactly ten minutes.

Yan can jump off a bridge, as far as I'm concerned. The rest of them better keep their distance.

The carnival is a sprawling beast of a site. More than half a mile in all directions of stands, tents and trailers. There's a Ferris wheel to collapse and load onto its truck; miles of electric cable to pull up and wind. Even with nearly a hundred of us swarming over the site like ants, it still takes us most of the day. We pack up the last truck with sore muscles and blistered hands, stomachs growling and throats dry.

"Load up." Robbie's voice echoes through the gathered crowd. He stands on a crate, his watchful eyes dragging over us. "We'll be driving through the night. Grab whatever snacks and shit you want now, because we're not stopping until we hit our next town."

It's always like this. Long, cramped hours stuffed in some smelly truck, scoffing chips and dying to pee. Fighting for control of the radio, or napping with the window vibrating our skulls. Robbie rules the convoy with an iron fist, and I guess I can see why. If even a few trucks started to dawdle, we'd be screwed at the other end.

One guy took a sneaky detour to Taco Bell last season and kept everyone waiting half an hour at the other end. Robbie fired him on the spot, smacking his taco out of his hand. I remember staring at the shredded lettuce in the grass and wondering why the hell you'd risk it all for *Taco Bell*.

We scatter, some darting to the bushes for a final leak while others rummage through the kitchen boxes for food. I sidle up behind Ginny, blowing her a kiss when she dumps a packet of chips and a soda in my arms.

"Got space for another?"

Usually, I ride with the other headliners in a minibus. But that would mean sitting near Aleksi, being reminded of Yan every time I glance over. Plus, there will be the pitying looks at my wrist. No, thank you.

And anyway, like Robbie said: I'm not a headliner right now.

"Sure thing, honey. Though if Robbie comes asking, this was all your idea."

"Deal."

I swipe an extra bag of chips and follow Ginny to her battered Honda Civic. The late afternoon light's fading, washing the little red car in a buttery glow. I throw myself into the passenger seat, kicking off my boots and propping my feet up on the dashboard. A sea of crumpled receipts and old straw wrappers litter the carpet below my feet, and a Christmas tree-shaped air-freshener dangles from the rear view mirror.

Ginny lowers herself into the driver's seat, rolling her eyes and batting at my feet.

She's just playing. Might as well be comfortable.

It's going to be a damn long drive.

* * *

"Where the hell did you skip off to?"

We're gathered under blood-red morning skies, laying the

ground for our new site. We could be here for weeks or even months, depending on Robbie's whim. As long as the crowds flow through the gates and cash leaves their pockets, there's no reason for us to move on. When we unload the trucks and set it all up, we have one chance to do it right.

I slept like shit last night, so I'm not at my most charming—just for a change. My purple hair is tangled and wild, thrown into a messy ponytail. There's nowhere hooked up for showers yet, so we're all stinking to high heaven, everyone aching and coated in yesterday's grime.

Yeah. I guess I can see why my mom wrinkles her nose when I come home. She's from another world, one filled with neatly pressed shirts and lacy napkins. Cirque de la Lune is rough living at the best of times.

"Huh?" I play dumb, looking around at my feet before raising an eyebrow at Robbie. He's glowering beside my elbow, dark shadows under his eyes from the drive. As the circus master, he's always the last to sleep and the first to rise. "I'm here, aren't I? What's the problem, Robert?"

It's damn near a crime to call Robbie by his full name, but he's pissing me off. Before Yan dropped me, Robbie barely spared me a glance except when he watched me during my set. Then, he stood and stared up at me just like all the other performers, his piercing gaze following my every move. It made my skin feel hot and tight, knowing his eyes were on me for those few minutes.

But since I set foot back in the carnival, Robbie's had it out for me. No more flying under the radar; I can't curse or rest my wrist for a second without his blue-eyed glare burning through my skin.

Robbie ignores my jab, his nostrils flaring. "Headliners ride

13

in the minibus. You know that, Harris."

"Headliners get their own trailers, too." I shrug sadly. "Life can be unpredictable."

"You—"

Whatever Robbie's about to say has to wait. A crash shakes the ground, echoing from the other side of the trucks, and Robbie curses and takes off running. Normally, I'd sprint towards the hollering too, but this morning I'm too damn tired. I shake my head and get back to work, laying cables for the stalls.

"Well, well. Look what we have here."

I'd know that voice anywhere: Kamran Lajani. When Kamran speaks, it's like warm, dripping honey sliding down my spine. Maybe it's all that fire-eating, warming up his throat.

"Piss off, Kamran."

I stare at my boots as I lay the cable. I'm clumsy one-handed, and it's way messier than I'd usually allow. Seeing my own sloppy work is making my eye twitch.

Kamran's chuckle is husky. "That's no way to greet an old friend."

I snort and eye him through the escaped strands of my hair. "It's too early for your bullshit. Run along."

Kamran's been here the longest of the headliners. He beats my three years hands down. In all that time, though, we've never become friends, though we've hung out plenty of times. There's something slippery about him that sets me on edge, makes the hairs rise on the back of my neck. With his blue-black curling hair and amber eyes, he's a trickster down to his handsome bones.

"You missed a spot there, darling."

I ignore him, flexing my fingers in my grubby cast. They

throb, but not so badly as before.

"How is it?" a low voice asks, and I glance up to find Aleksi watching me. He frowns at my cast like he can see through the plaster, his long brown hair fluttering in the breeze. His broad shoulders fill his white t-shirt, and his jeans cling to his muscular thighs.

Even after a full show, an overnight pack, and no shower this morning, he looks like the centerfold of a magazine.

I huff, not in the mood for chit-chat. "Ask your brother."

His shoulders tighten at that. Good. I'm trying to work, not host a tea party.

"Don't bother, Aleksi," Kamran purrs. "Hazel's in one of her moods, aren't you, darling?"

My good hand clenches around the cable and I wheel on the fire-eating asshole. He lounges against an open crate, amusement dancing in his eyes. They drop to my boots and rove back up my body, lingering on the tattoos on my thighs not covered by the hem of my shorts.

Heat prickles over my skin where his eyes have trailed. Fucking Kamran.

"Some of us are here to work," I say as snippily as I can, going back to laying my messy cable. I get so wrapped up in the task, I don't even notice Kamran darting behind me until it's too late.

"You're still wearing this? Oh, Hazel."

He dances away from my snatching hand, my locket dangling from his fingers. It's a gold heart on a fine chain—nothing special, but it's mine.

Yan gave it to me the first year I joined. I wore it so much it became a part of me. And even though I'm done with him, I still love my locket.

15

"Give that back."

I drop the cable and stalk after Kamran, but it's like trying to catch your own shadow. He's always just out of reach, a cruel smile tilting his lips.

He flicks the locket open and shows Aleksi the photo inside. It's an old one of Yan and me, his arms wrapped around me from behind. We look so young—I was barely eighteen in that photo—and I'm beaming so freaking wide.

Aleksi glances up at me, pity creasing his eyes.

My hand drops, my cheeks flushing crimson. What am I doing, chasing after that memory? It stopped meaning anything the night Yan threw it all away. The night he dropped me in the middle of a show, then told me in the hospital that he was leaving for another circus.

Leaving with Sasha, our third trapeze artist. Go fucking figure.

"Throw it. Whatever." I scrub a hand over my face, then swipe the hair back from my eyes. "Sell it. Use it as a stall prize. I don't fucking care."

I march back to my pile of cable, cursing the heat staining my skin. Who cares if these assholes think I'm pining? I don't give a shit what they think of me. One of them is Yan's brother, for Christ's sake, and the other I wouldn't trust with his hands tied behind his back.

They'll find someone new to torment soon. Someone who *wants* their attention.

Chapter 3

Five days of sawing, sweating and hammering later, we're ready to open the carnival gates. The rides are up, their engines whirring, and hot, sugary scents waft from the food stalls. We've done a supply run, restocking food and fuel, and street teams have hit up the local towns to spread the word.

We're ready. Settled and restless, hungry for fresh crowds. We want to dazzle and amaze; swindle and tease.

It's the promise of Cirque de la Lune. There's always a risk to coming to these grounds; that's what draws so many people in.

Our trailers cluster together on the far side of the grounds, hidden behind the big top tent. We don't let strangers wander through our living space; it ruins the magic. Plus, we trust the visitors about as much as they trust us. A townie would have to be pretty fucking nosy to find where we sleep.

Doesn't matter if they do. Robbie always keeps a few people on guard.

Everyone loves opening night in a new place. We open the gates and the crowds flood in, eyes bright and wide. They come to us for wonder, for fear, to feel something primal. And we give them all of those things in spades.

Usually, on opening night, I'd be slipping into my costume and painting my face with otherworldly makeup. I'd be swigging water and gnawing on handfuls of popcorn to steady my nerves, peeking out of a slit in the big top canvas to eye up the audience.

Not tonight. Tonight, I'm zipping up a goddamn skeleton onesie. It's black fleece, with a glow in the dark skeleton stuck on the front, the skull's jaw hanging open in a shriek.

Fucking Robbie. I knew I'd pay for calling him Robert.

"Everyone good?"

The man of the hour sticks his sandy blond head into the makeup trailer. He takes one look at me and throws his head back, letting out a hearty belly laugh.

Robbie McGreeves laughs maybe twice a year in my earshot. I'm honored to have inspired this outburst.

"Fucking fantastic, boss man." I tuck a stray lock of purple hair down my neckline. Once I slide the mask over my head and fasten it, there's not an inch of my skin on view. Already, I'm sweating buckets inside this damn costume, and it smelled ripe to begin with.

Lesson learned. Don't mess with Robbie. He'll only stick you on the worst job of all: jumping out at the kiddies in the haunted house.

Goddamn it. What a night.

Two hours in, it's exactly as awful as expected. The condensation from my breath has soaked into the fleece so that it clings wet to the front of my face. I've made dozens of kids and even a few adults scream, but it's a shit trade for being water-boarded by my own costume.

Robbie checks on me twice in the first hour. I jump out at him both times, but the bastard doesn't even flinch.

By the second hour, he's found better things to do. That's my cue.

The haunted house is one of those fold-out fairground rides, with creepy music playing on a loop. Visitors sit in a little train which winds its way through the rooms, past animatronic statues of witches and psycho killers, getting sprayed by fake blood. There's a hallway of warped, fun-house mirrors, and dry ice misting the floor.

It's dumb. So, so dumb. But the kids love it. That's the only reason Robbie keeps it in rotation, and the reason I'm stuck here tonight. Whoever has pissed Robbie off gets the honor of this stinking onesie.

Well, I've done my time. It's getting late, and that means fewer kids on the ride. I slip down the back of the deck, jumping down onto the grass. Sliding my mask to the top of my head, I take a lungful of crisp, autumn air.

I taste the smoke from the fire pits by the trailers, along with the flames of the fire eaters. It's colder here than our last town—we must have climbed higher into the mountains. I shiver in my thin onesie, only wearing a tank top and leggings underneath, my sweat cooling on my skin.

The brisk jog through the wet grass warms me right back up again. The big top tent is lit up from beneath, its doorway thronged with people. Through the opening, I can see the shadow of a performer flickering over the tent canvas.

I veer away from the main opening and keep jogging, passing the slit I went through when I first came back. Robbie stands there sometimes, and it's not worth pissing him off again. The only job worse than the haunted house is cleaning out the pop-up toilet blocks.

I circle all the way to the back of the tent until the trailers are on my right side. I keep to the shadows, never mind my glow-in-the-dark skeleton. I'm just here for a peek.

The warm air hits me like a wall when I duck inside. It's humid in the tent, heated from inside by the sweat of the performers, the gasps and whoops of the crowd. All these hot bodies cram in together to watch someone risk their life.

Jealousy curls like a hook in my gut. That should be me up there.

My bad wrist presses against my chest, the cast lumpy under the fleece. I hold it in my other hand and stare up at Aleksi as he plummets to the ground.

This is his signature move. He spins and climbs his way to the top of the silks, wrapping himself up like a present. Then he drops, unraveling so fast the audience shrieks, and catches himself a foot off the ground. I just about had a heart attack the first time I saw him do it. Even now, I bite my lip hard enough to bleed.

"Quite a sight, isn't it?"

Kamran hops onto a nearby speaker. The music from the live band thrums loud enough to rattle my teeth, but he doesn't even seem to notice as he rests back on his palms. He's dressed in his fire-eating costume—shirtless, with tight black pants and leather boots. Straps criss-cross over his muscled chest, and glitter sheens his skin.

He looks like he wandered out of a renaissance fair and got a job as a stripper.

"That's why he's headlining."

I drag my eyes away from Kamran's golden brown chest and glance back up at Aleksi. He makes it look so easy, like he's swimming through water rather than air. His long brown hair slides over his bare shoulders, his broad chest shining with sweat. Aleksi's pants are cream rather than black, cut off at the calf, and his feet are bare.

No bells and whistles. He doesn't need them. There's nothing to distract from the grace of his movement.

Kamran nudges me with the toe of his boot, and I shoot him a glare. His amber eyes crease, laughing at me, ringed thick with kohl. When he leans down to murmur in my ear, my locket swings off his chest and dangles before my eyes.

"What would dear Robbie say if he found you in here? Surely there are a few more sticky little children to spook in the haunted house."

Fuck. I chew on the inside of my cheek before grabbing Kamran's arm and tugging him close, speaking over the pounding of the band.

"Don't tell him."

"What will you give me in return?" He smirks, kicking his boots against the speaker.

I level him a look. "I prepaid this favor. That locket, remember?"

Kamran jerks his chin down, like he forgot the locket sparkling on his chest. When he pulls it over his head, it ruffles his dark curls up and smears his eyeliner on one side.

He waits for me to hold out my hand. I cock my head, lips curled in a smirk.

"Ugh. Why must everything be a battle with you?"

Kamran fastens the locket around my neck before I can blink. It drops to rest against the skeleton's breast bone, glinting in the tent's flickering lights.

I fiddle with it, studiously ignoring the asshole watching my every move. It takes some fumbling with my stupid fleece mittens, but I finally tease the damn thing open and then I suck

21

in a breath.

He's switched the photo. It's not Yan anymore—it's me and Ginny, slumped on each other and laughing with matching face paints. My throat is suddenly tight, and I cough to loosen it.

"I'm not giving you anything else," I tell Kamran. "I never wanted to give you this. Tell Robbie if you must, but know that it makes you a dick."

Kamran beams and hops down off the speaker, always so sprightly, landing about an inch from my toes. I rear back out of instinct, but he pinches the fleece of my onesie and keeps me on balance.

"Better not break the other wrist, darling." Kamran chucks me under the chin, making my mask slip over my eyes. "You're so grumpy when you're sore."

He sidles back into the crowd, his narrow hips full of sensual grace. I watch him go, surreptitiously sniffing the onesie to check how bad I smell.

The stink hits my nose, and I drop the fleece with a grimace.

I can't catch a break.

* * *

The last of the rabble clears out a while after midnight. They've had their fill of jugglers and acrobats; they've made themselves sick on cotton candy and juicy burgers. Once Robbie decides we're done for the night, they don't tend to linger. Why would they, when the performers disappear like smoke and the stalls begin to pack up?

I hop down the metal steps to the haunted house and lock up. My ride's been empty for over an hour—not many kids out this late—so I got a head start on sweeping and closing down. We're expected back at the fire pits to debrief and unwind in twenty minutes or so.

I know exactly what I'm going to do with my stolen time.

The grass whips at my ankles as I jog back to the big top tent, my breath freezing in foggy puffs. It's going to be a cold one. I hope Danika doesn't want to spoon.

The tent is dark and empty, the entrance pulled shut. I undo a few ties, slipping in through a doorway and cursing when my skeleton mask slides down my back and tries to choke me.

Yeah, this isn't happening again. If Robbie exiles me to the haunted house long term, I'm finding another damn costume.

The trapeze bar dangles lifeless over a small stage at the back. Usually, it'd be front and center, raised high overhead of the audience. But with Sasha and Yan ditching out, and my wrist getting banged up, there's no one here to use it. I don't know why Robbie bothered to have it set up at all, unless it was for me.

Huh. Guess the boss man is keen for me to practice.

That'd better be it, because the idea of him simply doing something nice makes my chest tight and my pulse hammer. I don't want his damn pity. I don't fucking need it.

I do, however, want a go on the trapeze.

My footsteps echo as I step up onto the stage. I unzip the onesie, shrugging the fleece sleeves off my shoulders and knotting them clumsily at my waist. The cold air washes over my skin, sending goosebumps prickling, but when I reach up and place my good palm on the trapeze bar, I flush hot.

Home. This is home. It's been so long.

I wiggle my fingers inside my cast, ignoring the dull ache of my bones. It's awkward, but I can just about wrap my fingertips

23

around the trapeze bar.

No way can I put weight on it, though. Stupid wrist.

I abandon that plan, dropping my injured hand and sliding the other to the center of the bar. Sucking in a breath, I slowly put all my weight on that arm. The stage creaks as my knees bend and my feet lift off the floor. I spin in the air, right hand gripping hard and my shoulder shaking with the effort.

Damn. I could do this in my sleep three weeks ago. How have I lost all of my fitness so quickly?

Little grunts escape through my teeth as I force myself through a set of pull ups. Sweat slides down my back, and my shoulder muscles burn.

My break is over. Time to get back to work.

"You're off balance."

The voice makes me jerk, and my sweaty grip slides off the bar. I drop like a stone, landing on my knees on the stage.

"Shit!" I curse and slump to one side, my knees throbbing hot. Aleksi steps out from behind the juggling platform, his mouth twisted into a grimace. "Are you trying to break my legs, too? You're as bad as your damn brother."

"Hardly."

Aleksi leaps onto the stage in one fluid motion. He squats beside me, prodding gently at my knees through the fleece. It hurts, but it's nothing like the agony of when I broke my wrist. Just bruises and injured pride. I sit rigid, catching a whiff of cinnamon and cloves when Aleksi's hair sweeps forward.

My stomach rumbles.

God.

"You were off balance." Aleksi raises his head, our faces just inches apart. He makes no effort to move back, and I don't push him away either. His brown eyes are so dark they're

24

almost black in the shadows of the tent. "You're hunching to protect your wrist. You need to relax your shoulders, or your form will be off."

I lick my lips. My knee-jerk reaction is to tell him to piss off, but Aleksi is the best aerial artist here. He knows what he's talking about, and honestly, I need all the help I can get.

"Is it how I'm holding it?"

He nods, visibly relaxing now that I've refrained from biting his head off.

"Try wrapping it in a sling next time. That way you can relax that whole side of your body."

It makes sense. I find myself nodding along, trying to figure out where I can snag some bandages. I don't even think when Aleksi straightens up and offers me his palm. I take it, my fingers winding around his wrist, and let him tug me to my feet.

My nose comes to the same level as his collarbone. Up close, even in the dark, I can see all the planes of his hard muscles. Aleksi is sculpted like a Greek statue, his body honed by his art.

"Thanks," I croak, and duck around him before hopping down to the dirt.

The last thing I need is to get all warm and fuzzy over Aleksi Genkov. He and Yan are tight as thieves—there's no way he didn't know about Sasha. About the two of them training behind my back; about what Yan was planning.

I slide my onesie sleeves back on as I slip out through the canvas, suddenly chilled to the bone.

* * *

"How goes the haunted house? Have you found your calling?"

I force a grin as I throw myself down on Ginny's garden bench at the fire pits. The impact makes the flimsy bench wobble, and she holds her cup of mystery drink over my lap in case it spills.

Knowing Ginny, whatever is in that cup could eat through metal. Better not drip it on my thighs.

"You know me. I love scaring the shit out of strangers."

Ginny cackles, pressing her drink into my hand to hold while she rolls a cigarette. Tobacco stains coat the tips of her gnarled fingers, and though her knuckles are swollen and stiff, she's done in less than ten seconds.

"It's not forever, love."

She leans forward, the bench creaking as she dangles the tip of her cigarette in the flames. It gives me a chance to crane my neck, looking to see whether Aleksi followed me. Whether he'll tell Robbie what he caught me doing.

No sign of the acrobat. Ginny sits back with a grunt, and I turn around.

"It's bullshit. Jumping out at little kids and trying not to die from the stink of this costume."

Ginny leans in and sniffs the shoulder of my onesie, her nostrils whistling. She shrugs, brushing a speck of dirt off the fleece.

"Smells fine to me."

Yeah, I bet. Honestly, that's a low bar.

Robbie hauls himself onto an upturned barrel, and we settle, the chatter fading away. These meetings are short and sweet, and besides—no one dares disrespect the boss by talking over him.

No one except Ginny, apparently. Ten minutes in, she leans

over until her shoulder brushes mine. She mumbles out of the corner of her mouth, barely moving her lips.

"If you decide it's bullshit upfront, then it definitely will be. Try to enjoy it before you write it off, girl."

Robbie glowers at us, the firelight dancing over his face like some ancient tribesman. I offer him a weak smile, inching away from Ginny on the bench.

"Challenge accepted," I murmur through closed lips when Robbie finally turns away.

He wants me scaring little kids for a job?

I'll make them piss their tiny pants.

Chapter 4

Robbie waits three days to drop the bombshell on me. The workers are clustered round the fire pits on a Monday night—Monday's always an early finish. There's too much nagging at the back of the townies' minds: work deadlines and hair appointments. Things speed up here towards the end of the week, when people come to let loose and forget.

I've somehow found myself with Kamran at my side, while Aleksi sits across the fire. Danika's here too, along with a couple of the new stand workers. They cycle in and out, never staying long—except for the old-timers like Ginny, that is. Before Robbie founded Cirque de la Lune, she worked carnivals in Europe; in Latin America; on cruise ships.

She's the exception, not the rule. Most people make it through a season, if that.

Everyone wants a taste of the circus.

But plenty of them spit it back out.

The fire pits are dotted between the trailers, with a dozen or so gathered around each. We pull up lawn chairs, footstools, upturned buckets—anything to keep our asses out of that grass. A few pits away, someone's dragged a whole armchair set over.

More fool them when it rains. And judging by the dark

clouds snuffing out the stars, the heavens will open soon enough.

"Harris."

I don't know when Robbie started calling me by my surname, but I don't fucking like it. All it does is remind me of Ohio, of Mom and Dad, and of the disappointed set to their mouths whenever I'm there.

"Robert."

I raise an eyebrow at the boss where he's stepped up to Aleksi's shoulder. He frowns, crossing his arms over his broad chest. Considering he's not one of the performers, Robbie's as strong as anyone here.

"You're training with Aleksi."

Straight to the point, then. I can work with that.

"No, I'm not."

I can see the muscle leaping in his square jaw, even from all the way over here. The firelight bounces off his eyes, making him look otherworldly for a split second.

"I wasn't asking. Train up or get out."

Shit. It's not like I'm not training—I've been up at dawn every morning, stretching out my seized muscles and working through body-weight drills. Only a handful of the other headliners are that committed, and they're performing every damn night.

"Aleksi does silks," I point out. "Trapeze is different."

The man in question sits in stony silence, listening to us argue over his head.

I don't know what got Robbie in such a twist, but he's not having any of it tonight.

"Aleksi knows plenty. Hell, he's probably better than you and it's not even his specialty."

I sink down in my lawn chair, the cold metal biting into the back of my neck. Even though I work to keep my face blank, my chest clenches like I'm having a heart attack.

That's it. That's exactly what I fear; the thing that drags me awake each morning in a cold sweat.

What if I'm not good enough? What if the whoops of the audience were for Yan all along?

Aleksi shoots Robbie an annoyed glance, but I'm done with this conversation. I need to get away from here, get on my own and work through the pounding of my heart. I clear my throat and give a jerky nod, not meeting anyone's eye. Not Robbie's, not Aleksi's, and not Kamran's—even as he nudges my side.

"Fine."

After what feels like a year, Robbie finally huffs and stomps off to ruin someone else's night. I count to sixty in my head so it doesn't look like I'm running away, then I push to my feet.

"It's going to rain," I mumble, and set off towards my trailer. Everyone else looks up, squinting at the clouds, then the whispering starts behind my back. I grit my teeth and ignore it, striding faster through the grass.

"Forget him."

I whip my head to the side and find Kamran easily keeping pace. He doesn't even seem to rush, his long legs eating up the ground. For once, he's not laughing or prodding at me, his serious gaze focused on my trailer.

I loose a breath. "Forget who?"

Kamran's lips quirk. "Precisely."

He walks me all the way to my trailer steps, then stares down at me like he expects something. What, does he need a medal for not being an ass for two entire minutes?

"Thank you for walking me home," I tell him sweetly, jutting my hip and splaying my uninjured hand over my heart. "It's so awful scary out here in the dark."

Kamran snorts, that intense gaze vanishing, and I'm both relieved and disappointed. But then he leans down, his warm breath tickling at my ear.

"Any time, Hazel, darling. The only person I want snatching you is me."

* * *

I've been here for more than a week. I can't put it off for much longer.

I sit on the edge of my bed, my feet planted on the floor, and tap my phone against my palm.

God, I hate these phone calls. There's so much bitterness—from everyone involved.

The clock changes, the numbers flickering on the screen, and I suck in a deep breath and hold it, counting to ten. When it feels like my lungs will burst, I gust it out again.

I feel a tiny bit better as I scroll through my contacts. Yan taught me that breathing trick as a way to settle stage nerves, and though he can obviously burn in hell, the trick still comes in handy.

Going on stage in front of roaring crowds is nothing compared to this. My palms are damp with sweat as I hold the phone up to my ear.

It rings on and on, the tinny jangling sound mocking me. They always do this—they always leave me hanging for twenty seconds first. I used to hang up, too pissed off to wait, but it wasn't worth the fall out.

They can play their mind games if they must. I just want to

get this over with.

"Hello?"

This is another part of it. Even though we set a time in advance, they still pretend they don't know who's calling. Mom answers—after sufficient rings—then acts surprised I've actually called when I promised.

Without fail, Dad will be in the garden or out washing the car. Anything to avoid me thinking they're eager to hear from me.

"Hi, Mom."

"Oh, Hazel! We weren't sure you'd call."

I grind my teeth, pinching the bridge of my nose.

"Well, I said I would."

"Yes, of course. Such a lovely surprise."

My parents are masters of passive aggression.

"Is Dad there?" I ask, already knowing the answer.

"He just stepped out to do some work on the rose bushes. Hold on one moment, Hazel, I'll just duck my head out and see if he's free."

I close my eyes as she sets the phone down, her footsteps echoing down the handset. There's about a fifty-fifty chance that Dad will bother to come inside.

Mom favors thinly veiled criticism and snide comments to get her point across. Left to his own devices, Dad likes to shut me out completely.

You'd think I was a felon or a drug addict from the disappointment flowing down the phone in waves. Not a legitimate performer who earns her own way.

But then, my parents would prefer that I live off them than do this. Hell, Dad's big dream for me was that I'd marry some suit in his company and squeeze out three kids before I hit thirty.

Not that there's anything wrong with that. It's just not my path.

Mom's out of breath when she picks up the phone.

"I'm afraid your father's a little tied up. He's in the middle of some delicate pruning."

"Jesus," I say, wincing as Mom hisses in disapproval. "Sounds serious."

"Yes, well perhaps next time you could call when he's not too busy."

I can't help myself. My irritation bursts out, my voice raising. As I half-yell, gesturing at the wall, Danika opens the trailer door and steps inside.

"You picked the time! I called when you wanted! All you had to do was pick up the damn phone."

Danika raises her eyebrows, eyes flicking to me with naked curiosity as she crosses to her bed. I screw my eyes shut again and try to rein my temper back.

"Really, Hazel," Mom's saying. "Perhaps you should see a doctor again. These outbursts are not normal."

I hang up, jabbing the button on my screen before I say something I really regret. Tossing the phone onto my quilt, I clench my hands into my hair and pull until my eyes water.

"Parents?" Danika asks quietly.

I shoot her a venomous look, then sigh. My body slumps, my shoulders rounding forward, and my hands drop into my lap.

"Who else?"

Danika nods, pausing on her way back out.

"Can't choose them. Can stop calling them, though."

I start to argue but pause with my mouth hanging open. She's right.

The trailer door swings closed behind her, the strains of laughter outside fading away.

* * *

Our only free time is the mornings. Afternoons are swallowed up by chores and supply runs; by repairs and construction projects. And in the evenings, our gates open. So the hours between breakfast and midday, when everyone else is napping or reading or getting some damn alone time—that precious stretch of my time belongs to Aleksi Genkov now.

Perfect.

"I'm not happy about this."

"You don't say."

We start bickering as soon as I enter the tent. I come through the front entrance for once, crossing the trampled dirt to the little trapeze stage. You can see that nothing happens here—the grass is thicker, less squashed by the audience's feet. The ground in front of Aleksi's platform is scuffed bare.

He stands on the stage, fiddling with the cables to raise the bar a few inches higher. Tangled in a heap by his sneakers is a practice harness.

"I'm not wearing that," I say flatly. I'm a goddamn professional, not a kid at a circus skills class.

"Yes, you are." Aleksi nudges it towards the edge of the stage with the toe of his shoe, not even glancing down from his task. "You don't have your strength back yet, or your form. If you get hurt again on my watch, Robbie will blame me—and he'd be right."

I breathe out hard through my nose, snatching up the harness.

It's ancient, caked in dust. That's how much the headliners bother with practice equipment. That's how much of an insult this is.

The thing is, it's not just about ego. It's about mindset.

If I start thinking I need a harness, putting one on every day, will I ever take it off again?

Against my better judgement, I voice that last question out loud. Aleksi finally looks at me, understanding dawning in his eyes.

"You will. I'll take it away myself."

Ugh. Fine. He's so damn reasonable.

Aleksi Genkov is a lot of other things, too, even right after breakfast. His skin is bright and fresh, scrubbed clean—Kamran told me once Aleksi likes to swim in nearby rivers. God knows if that's true—Kamran weaves a pretty tale—but it suits Aleksi, somehow.

His long hair is loose over his shoulders, like always, and his movements are precise and calm. He looks damn good in his jeans and moss green sweater, too, rolled up to showcase his arms.

Me? My hair is still wet from the shower, which was awkward and hurried with my arm stuffed in a plastic bag. When I step out of my sweats, my workout shorts show the bruises on my knees. I've had plenty of comments about those particular bruises, and at least one roadie has walked away with a broken nose.

It's freezing, even with the remnants of last night's humidity, but I tug my sweatshirt off and stand there in just shorts and a vest. I need as much bare skin as possible, so I'm not slipping around on the bar. My cast is grubbier than ever, and if you get too close, you can smell the trapped sweat.

Yeah, I've got no business eyeing up Aleksi Genkov.

"Ready?"

I nod and step into the harness, pulling it up my thighs without a word. I fumble with the buckles, my fingers awkward in the cast, and Aleksi takes over, strapping me in. His fingers brush my hips and thighs as he pulls the harness tight, and I hold my breath, trying not to inhale the delicious scent of his hair.

Heat pools between my legs, and I glare down at my crotch. Fucking traitor.

I may be injured, but Aleksi doesn't hold back. He puts me through my paces until I'm breathing hard and my skin's slick with sweat, wrapping my arm up in a sling part way so I can work on keeping proper form. It's hard enough doing this shit two-handed, but with only one arm I burn out fast. I start to tell him I'm done for the day, but his firm hands wrap around my waist.

"I'll take your weight. Go through the static holds."

We can't swing back and forth, obviously, but there are plenty of moves for a static bar. I work through them as best I can, my mind flipping between whining about the ache in my wrist and screaming about Aleksi's hands on my body. I didn't get half so distracted by Yan, and I was dating the guy.

I finally manage to spin around the bar and hold a handstand, my legs pointing straight towards the canvas ceiling. Slow claps echo through the tent, and I lower jerkily into Aleksi's arms.

Kamran and Robbie stand in the entrance, Ginny beaming at their side. It's Kamran clapping, a smirk curling his lips, while Robbie watches us intently, arms crossed.

Ginny cups her hands around her mouth. "Wonderful, Hazel!

This Genkov boy is an upgrade."

I flush bright red, heat burning my cheeks, and shove at Aleksi to put me down. He starts unbuckling my harness without another word. I guess practice is over.

I turn back to our audience, frazzled. "Happy, boss man?" I call, voice too high.

Robbie frowns at Aleksi's bent head where he's pulling the harness loose at my thigh.

"Very happy," he clips out, then spins on his heel and walks off.

Kamran tips back his head and laughs, a throaty sound, like he's in on a joke all by himself.

"Come find me later, Hazelnut."

He offers Ginny his elbow, then they're gone too. I've been alone with Aleksi all morning, but it's suddenly awkward, the silence loaded and tense. The harness drops to the stage, pooling around my feet, and Aleski takes my hand as I step out.

Like I didn't just balance one-handed on the bar. Like I'm some historical duchess.

"Thanks," I blurt out, before I can say anything worse. Aleksi drops my hand, and his fingers tap at the side of his thigh. "This actually helped a lot. You're a great teacher."

He nods, his cheekbones flushing light pink.

Well. That's adorable.

For an insane moment, I want to run my fingers through his soft hair. My hand twitches towards him, like he's mine to touch like that, like I didn't just have my heart trampled by his brother.

I snatch my hand back, flushing pink to match.

"See you later."

I leap down from the stage and hightail it out of there. Halfway across the grass to my trailer, I realize I forgot my sweats and sneakers.

Forget it. I can't go back there. I'll dig them out of the lost and found later when there's no risk of making a fool of myself.

* * *

I don't have to go sniffing about for my stuff in the end. Aleksi finds me after lunch, setting up the haunted house. There's not all that much to do, beyond opening everything up, checking the power, and doing a walk-through of all the effects. I refill some of the automatic sprinklers so the kids will get a good shot of fake blood. I even try and buff some of the warped fun house mirrors, but I run out of jobs before the first hour is up.

So, I slide into the haunted train, prop my feet on the safety bar, and watch everyone else swarm over the grounds. The stalls are unlocked and opened, their chalkboard signs folding out. The grills and water boilers are coaxed to life, fresh onions chopped and coffee put on to roast.

To an outsider, this would look manic. The yells of the vendors echo to one another; the roadies jog to and fro across the site. Robbie's out there too, striding around and barking instructions into his radio.

It may look chaotic, but there's a method to the madness. Look closer, and you see it's an intricate dance, with every single worker knowing their own role by heart.

Case in point: I've got fuck-all to do for the next few hours.

Kamran and the other performers spread out on the grass, warming up and prepping their equipment. There are jugglers, mimes on stilts, puppeteers, contortionists. Kamran's checking over his fire-eating gear, his fine ass already in his costume. Sadly, it's too cold for his bare chest yet, and he's wearing what looks like a gray fishing sweater. The neckline dips below his collarbone, hanging loose on his shoulders—the wool clearly stretched. His firm, sculpted chest peeks through, and I find myself watching him more than anyone else.

"You left these."

I jump about a foot in the air, bashing my elbow on the side of the train. Aleksi stands on the haunted house deck, holding a pile of my neatly folded sweatshirt and pants, my sneakers resting on top. He frowns at where I'm rubbing my elbow, his hands tightening on my stuff.

"Thanks," I mutter, reaching over before he creases all his pretty folds. I shrug the sweatshirt straight on over my cardigan, poking my cast through the sleeve.

I wait for him to go, but Aleksi just stands there watching me. Finally, I nod at the seat beside mine.

"Wanna watch?"

He nods and climbs in beside me.

The train is built for little kids mostly—it's a squeeze to fit us both in. Our thighs press together, the heat of his legs searing through his jeans and my leggings. After a moment, he digs two packets of toffee out of his jeans and hands me one.

"What are you dressing as tonight?" he asks quietly, eyes on the food stands.

I grumble at the reminder. The haunted house costumes are shit, no way around it.

"Maybe a witch," I muse. "Or maybe I'll just wear shorts and scare the kids with my bruises."

Aleksi grunts, watching as Kamran swallows a ball of fire. Sweat gleams on his brown chest beneath his fishing jumper, and I shift on the plastic bench. Except it presses me firmer against Aleksi's muscled thigh, and now I'm squirming for a different reason.

Aleksi turns his head and finally looks at me. His hair swings forward in a curtain, cutting us off from view.

His eyes drop to my mouth, and I bite my lip.

Fuck. This is happening? Fuck.

I lean forward, the plastic creaking around me, but a buzzing noise makes me jump back. Aleksi swears and digs his phone out of his pocket, clicking the screen off quickly when he sees who it is.

Too late. I saw Yan's face, grinning at me from the screen. It's a bucket of cold water, and I fumble my way out of the train seat.

"Hazel." Aleksi reaches for me, his mouth turned down. I snatch my hand out of reach and scoop up my sweats and sneakers, hopping off the deck onto the grass.

I'm all set up. Ready to rock. No reason to linger, especially not with him.

"Trouble in paradise?" Kamran calls as I walk past, but I'm not in the mood. I flip him off without looking and go straight to my trailer, my throat tight.

"Oh." I throw the door open and find Danika blinking back. "I forgot about you."

She sighs, rolling her eyes and swinging her legs off her bed, and I feel like a prize bitch. Sure, I want to be alone right now, so much that I could scream. But she lives here too, thanks to fucking Robbie, and my personal shit isn't her problem.

"Wait." I hold up a palm. "You don't have to go. I'm just being an asshole."

"What's new?" Danika snipes, but she settles back on her

bed. I linger in the doorway for a moment before closing it gently behind me.

"Here." I toss Aleksi's unopened toffees onto her comforter. "Call it a peace offering."

Danika narrows her eyes at the packet like they might be poisoned. I cross the trailer and collapse on my bed.

Fuck. I toss an arm across my face, closing my eyes. I can't believe I nearly kissed Aleksi.

The crinkle of foil interrupts my pity party, and I smile into my arm.

These guys might be assholes. Doesn't mean *I* have to be one.

Chapter 5

Halloween night is a major event in the haunted house. It's the one night of the year this poky little ride's not an afterthought; the one night it's the main attraction. The townies make a beeline straight here from the gates, their little kids dragging buckets of trick-or-treat candy along the ground.

I hate to admit it, but I'm secretly getting invested in the haunted house. I'm still working out alone every morning at dawn, then training with Aleksi after breakfast. Trapeze is still the priority, the true reason I'm here.

I'm lost when my feet touch back on the ground and I'm forced to muddle through the rest of my day. I help out Ginny and the other stall workers, or slink off to my trailer for a nap. But the big top tent calls to me, especially when it's lit up and bustling with roaring crowds at night.

For Halloween, though, it's all about the haunted house. I have ideas. They start with my epic Zombie Bo Peep costume, and end with a whole truckload of fake cobwebs, toy spiders, red corn syrup blood, and dry ice. Tonight, I'm dialing this ancient ride up to eleven.

Screw it. Robbie wants me working in the haunted house? It'll be the creepiest damn house these kids have ever seen. I crank the spooky music up to the maximum volume, and arrive twenty minutes before the gates open to limber up before the crowds stream inside.

"I've seen you stretch less for the trapeze."

I glance down from where I'm lunging on the deck, my torn pink skirts billowing between my legs. Kamran grins up at me, rocking on his heels with his hands shoved into his pockets. He's dressed as a medieval court jester, complete with curly shoes, a crimson waistcoat, and one of those hats with dangly bells.

"What can I say? I'm an athlete."

Kamran chuckles, leaping onto the deck in one step. He falls into a lunge beside me, stretching one arm across his chest.

"You're right, as ever. The haunted house is serious stuff."

It's been dark for hours, the stars bright pinpricks in the sky, and the bursts of flames from the other fire-eaters light up patches of the grounds. Kamran should be down there, oiling his throat or whatever he does before a performance, not up here teasing me.

"Shouldn't you be gargling lighter fluid or something?"

Kamran clasps his hands together and stretches them to the sky, tilting into a back-bend. The bells tinkle on his hat, his dark hair curling around the brim.

"Can't you hear it? I have a tickle." His voice *is* kind of scratchy. "I requested a new post for the night."

I guess the last thing you should do to a sore throat is shove a fireball down it. Even so, my shoulders creep towards my ears. I straighten up, tugging at my blood-spattered skirts.

"No. Absolutely not. I've got this ride covered."

Kamran smiles at me, his face upside-down.

"On the busiest night of the year?"

Crap. This has Robbie written all over it. I grind my teeth and turn to glare out at the carnival grounds. They're dotted with glowing lanterns and the bright wash of floodlights. Rides are lit up and whirling, their tinned music blaring through speakers. Robbie could be anywhere out there, and he won't listen even if I find him.

Kamran straightens up. "Is it so terrible to work with me for one night?" He places his hands on my shoulders and ducks his head, squinting into my eyes. "You don't have to fight at every step for the sake of it, you know."

I hate that he's right. I brush his hands off my shoulders and point him at the box of decorations.

"Go round one more time with those, then. If you're so desperate to help."

"Oh, I am." Kamran strolls to the box and balances it easily on one palm. "I'm positively yearning, Hazelnut."

"Don't call me that," I snap, but he's already ducked through the shadowed doorway. I huff, picking up my skirts, and follow the tinkling of bells.

* * *

I've never spent much time with Kamran before. I'm not sure why. He's always seemed so wily, like he'd cheerfully trick me out of the shirt on my back. He's a master of sleight of hand, but besides my locket, he's never stolen from me.

He and Yan never got along. I guess that's why. They used to circle each other like two spitting cats. That seems like a really dumb reason, now. Any rival of Yan's is a friend of mine.

It turns out, after three hours running the haunted house together, that Kamran is really fucking fun. He just doesn't give a shit. He flirts with every adult he loads into the train, regardless of age or gender, and he's so goofy with the kids that they scream out for him when they leave. I've never seen someone so unselfconscious. Kamran wouldn't know an inhibition if it bit him in the ass.

I chew the inside of my cheek. It's kind of sexy.

Even though he's not fire-eating tonight, Kamran's eyes are still ringed with thick kohl. His amber irises are startling when they catch the light, and I find myself watching his face just for those moments.

I watch his plump, sensual lips, too. His sharp cheekbones. The blue sheen to his dark, curling hair.

Okay, Kamran is a walking work of art. I can admit it. I hadn't noticed before tonight, maybe because we'd never spent this much time together. Never been alone.

We're alone now. Well, except for the trainloads of screaming kids.

"Rah!"

Kamran jumps out at them just as the sprinklers mist the train with fake blood. The kids scream and even the adults jerk back, cursing under their breath; Kamran and I melt back into the shadows, grinning ear-to-ear.

"You should use that voice you use when Mick burns the coffee." Kamran places his lips by my temple, his warm breath tickling my skin. "Now that's scary."

I elbow him, but he doesn't move away. If anything, he crowds closer. Kamran presses me against the haunted house wall, the tip of his nose dragging through my hair. I grab his shoulders to push him away, but find myself tugging him closer. He hums, plastering his whole body against me—every muscle, every dip and hollow.

45

"This is interesting." His scratchy voice sounds breathless. "Do you want me too, Hazelnut?"

I nip at his earlobe, heart thundering in my chest. "Call me that again and I'll stuff those bells where the sun don't shine."

Kamran hisses like I've whispered sweet nothings, and I feel the hard line of his cock against my hip. I can't help myself—I roll my body against it, making him shudder and clench one hand in my hair.

What the hell am I doing? I haven't touched anyone—haven't let them touch me—since Yan, nearly two months ago. I swore I wouldn't fall into this trap again, wouldn't mix work and pleasure. I promised myself I wouldn't risk that kind of public humiliation again.

These thoughts run through my brain, even as Kamran seals his mouth to mine. I groan and lunge up, winding my arms around his neck, and swaying on the toes of my boots. Yan never kissed me like this—like I was the most delicious dessert he'd ever tasted. Kamran licks into my mouth like he can't get enough, like this is his only chance to sate his hunger.

The next train rattles around the corner and we jerk apart, chests heaving. I'm aching and slippery between my legs, my core uncomfortably swollen. What I wouldn't give to push Kamran to his knees, toss my skirts over his head, and put him to work.

I jump out at the train instead, not faking my grimace and wide eyes.

This wasn't part of the plan.

I avoid Kamran like the plague for the rest of the night, ducking out of one doorway as soon as he enters another. When we have to be together, I make sure we're out on the deck where everyone can see.

I don't trust myself alone with him. Not in the shadows, where there's nothing to stop us reaching for each other again.

"Hazel…"

He tries to talk to me for the thousandth time as we finish locking up. I twist the padlock onto the haunted house doors, sealing it shut for the night.

"Let's go," I mutter, jumping down onto the grass and heading for the trailers. Kamran gusts out a sigh but follows me, his inky hair clinging to his neck with sweat.

We're two of the last to arrive at the fire pits, standing far apart with our arms crossed. Robbie and Aleksi both frown at us, the boss from atop his barrel and Aleksi from a folding lawn chair. Their eyes dart between Kamran's clenched jaw and my flushed cheeks, absorbing way too much information.

Whatever. I widen my eyes at Robbie, willing him to get this over with.

Fantastic night, strong profits, yada yada yada. Two assholes wound up wrestling in the mud by the beer tent—nothing new.

I'm off and marching towards my trailer before Robbie's done bidding us all goodnight.

The metal steps squeak under my boots, and I slam the door shut behind me. Resting my shoulder blades against the door, I soak in the blissful quiet.

Danika will be a long time yet. She likes to sit and have a smoke after the carnival grounds close, playing cards with the roadies before bed.

Works for me. There's something I need to take care of.

I kick off my boots by the door and tug at the zipper of my Bo Peep dress. It catches halfway and I snarl, tugging hard until the fabric tears.

That'll work. I wriggle free of the dress, making a mental

47

note to darn the rip tomorrow and letting it pool on the floor. My sheets are cool when I slide into bed, tugging the quilt up to my chin.

Danika should be a few hours, but I don't want to give her an eyeful, just in case.

I close my eyes and lean back against the pillow, my uninjured hand sliding under my bralette. I squeeze one breast, tweaking the nipple before moving to the other side.

Kamran. The weight and heat of him pressed against me; his smoky chuckle in my ear. The way he kissed me, chest rumbling with a groan, his cock hard against my body. I've been on fire with it ever since, my blood molten in my veins.

My hand smooths down my stomach and slips into my underwear. I could take them off properly, but then I'd have to admit what I'm doing. Touching myself and wishing my hand belonged to Kamran Lajani.

No, thank you. I just need to scratch this itch. I dip my fingers down to my pussy, gathering the wetness there before circling my clit. I rub hard, bordering on rough, like I'm punishing myself for getting this wound up about Kamran at all. It doesn't take long until my back bows against the bed, my heels digging into the mattress.

If that train hadn't come around the corner—if we'd been alone just a few minutes longer—

My pussy clenches and my muscles twitch. Pressure gathers in my core, building as I screw my eyes shut and picture Kamran's clever hands parting my thighs. His black curls would tickle my skin, and his amber eyes would glint as he licked me from ass to clit. Perhaps he'd call me darling, his sly mouth curling into a smirk.

I'm so close. A whimper escapes my lips, my chest heaving

hard. Then... I picture Aleksi's hands too, gripping my waist like he does in training. I imagine him leaning over me, wafting that cinnamon and cloves scent, but it's a Scottish voice that speaks in my ear.

"Come for us, Hazel."

I shatter, biting the pillow to muffle my scream.

* * *

"This is a damn treasure trove."

Ginny digs through the sacks of costumes, fresh from the town laundromat. As the current circus dogsbody, it fell to me to drive the sacks of sweaty, musty costumes into town the morning after Halloween. I waited for hours in a poky laundromat—one that I'm pretty sure doubled up as a Chinese take-out—loading and unloading rows of machines with one hand.

I got a few looks from the townies. For my purple hair, my tattoos, my cast. More than anything, for the metric ton of ancient Halloween costumes I'd taken to be washed.

What, did they think that was my weekly wardrobe? Get a grip.

By the time I loaded up Ginny's battered old car and drove back to the grounds, I was bored out of my mind. But Robbie waved me straight from the makeshift parking lot to the make-up trailer to hang it all up.

No rest for the wicked. Fine, then. I set to work, fumbling wire coat hangers through sleeves, cursing and bumping around the trailer. When Ginny stuck her head through the doorway, I was breathing hard and sweating.

"They're ancient," I tell her.

49

"They're retro." Ginny winks. "Like me."

She pulls a blue feather boa off a hanger and drapes it round her shoulders. As a pile of her personal favorites grows on the counter top, I'm beginning to understand the state of her wardrobe a bit more.

"How was the big night in the haunted house? Are you still hating it?"

I shrug, wrestling a bed sheet ghost costume onto a hanger.

"Not anymore. And it was kind of fun. I'm getting into it, like you said."

I don't mention Kamran, or the way he pressed against me in the shadows. Ginny's so open minded her brain might fall out, but she's still like an aunt to me. Talking to her about guys—and gritting my teeth through the inevitable safety pointers—well, I don't need that torture.

Ginny jams a cowboy hat on her head.

"Told you I'm wise. If only the rest of these idiots would listen to me, this carnival would be heaven on earth."

I snort, tossing another empty sack onto the heap. Ginny has some pearls of wisdom, sure, but she also told me once that she lived for eight years in a cult. Any life advice from the hot dog vendor should be taken with a boatload of salt.

Time passes quicker with Ginny helping, though she siphons more costumes off to her personal stash than she hangs up on the rail. I watch her out of the corner of my eye when she picks up my skeleton onesie, but my shoulders relax when she sticks a hanger through the sleeves.

What can I say? I've gotten attached. Especially now it doesn't stink to high heaven.

Robbie pokes his head through the door as we're working through the last sack, and though he rolls his eyes at Ginny's outright thievery, he walks away without a word.

Good. Nothing to say means no complaints.

Told him I'd earn my keep.

* * *

"Adjust your grip. Good."

The last thing I need in training a few days later is Aleksi directing my grip. He's so sparing with his words, only ever murmuring instructions. There's no chat about the weather, or last night's show, or Yan.

He's purely professional. Quiet but stern.

It's killing me.

The memory of what I did on Halloween night leaves me shaky and flushed. Every time he touches me, nudging my limbs to correct my form, pressing down on my tense shoulders to make me relax—I shudder.

Aleksi snatches his hands back, a slight frown creasing his forehead, but it's not what he thinks.

It's not that I don't want him touching me. It's that I don't want him to stop. Halloween night opened some kind of dam inside me, and now I'm panting after him like I'm on heat.

I hang below the bar, knees bent, gritting my teeth through the ache in my wrist. The smelly cast is finally gone, my poor wrist emerging shrunken and ghostly white. I've got exercises to work through and a stress ball to squeeze, but I need more than that.

I need to get back on the trapeze.

I flex my fingers on the bar, dusted with white chalk. All my weight is still on my good hand; I'm just testing out the grip. My injured hand feels clumsy—like I slept on it and woke up with a dead limb.

"Breathe." Aleksi strokes a fingertip over the top of my injured hand. His brown eyes watch me closely, darting between my bitten lip and lowered eyebrows. "It's only your first day of rehab. Relax."

I gust out a breath and drop my feet to the floor, straightening up.

He's right. I know he is. But still…

"What if it doesn't come back?" Aleksi says nothing, waiting for me to elaborate. I lick my lips and toy with the trapeze bar. "What if I'm done?"

When Aleksi speaks, his quiet calm is gone. He's fierce, squeezing the trapeze cable in his fist until his knuckles turn white as he bites out the words.

"You're not done."

We've moved closer, somehow, over the last few seconds. Only the bar is between us, our feet nearly touching. He's close enough that I can see the freckles dusting his broad nose; the sooty eyelashes on his brown eyes. I sway forward, moving slowly like I'm in a dream. This is such a fucking bad idea, I know that, but I can't—I won't—stop myself.

It doesn't matter. Robbie stops us for me.

"How's it going?" he calls from the tent entrance, stepping in from the cold. He crosses the scraggly grass, his all-knowing eyes taking in our raw expressions; our hands on the bar; our faces just inches apart. Aleksi steps back, clearing his throat, and I roll my eyes.

"Incredible, boss man. First day without a cast and I'm ready for the big time."

I can't outright tell him to piss off, but I sure can make my feelings clear. Robbie has made my life nothing but difficult since I hurt my wrist. And he's so fucking observant, I can't look him in the eye with Halloween night still so fresh. It was his voice, low and gruff in my ear, that made me come so hard my ears rang.

He steps onto the stage, his boots echoing in the quiet, and I suddenly take a fresh interest in the buckles on my harness. I check them all one by one with shaking fingers while Aleksi and Robbie murmur to each other in hushed voices.

"…Doesn't need a partner," Aleksi mutters, and my head jerks up.

"What?"

Robbie smirks. "Look who's decided to join us."

I ignore him, staring at Aleksi. No partner? I've always had a partner. Yan practically trained me over the last few years. I've never done a solo routine, never even tried one, and the math isn't difficult. When you have half the performers on stage, they need to be twice as good.

Right now, I can't even hold my own weight with my injured hand. And I'm supposed to take center stage? Headline solo like Aleksi?

Come on.

Robbie's on the same page as me. His gaze flicks over my body, his expression doubtful as he takes in my bedraggled hair, my bruised legs, my throbbing wrist. I'm in a damn safety harness, for Christ's sake. I look about twelve.

"Show me."

The command clips out, and I'm moving before I even think about it. Robbie has that effect. He's so used to having every order obeyed, that his utter confidence bleeds over and you don't even think about questioning.

Well, I do, sometimes. Mostly to fuck with him.

But not when it comes to the trapeze. This is too important.

My wrist already aches, throbbing hot under my skin, but I step up to the bar and stretch my fingers.

"What do you want to see?" I ask, and I hate that my voice comes out husky.

Fucking Halloween night. What was I thinking?

Aleksi answers for him. "Move through the static holds." He glances at Robbie. "I'll need to take her weight."

Robbie shakes his head, stepping forward.

"I'll do it."

Um. What? I grip the bar with shaking hands, grunting as pain shoots through my wrist. As I drag myself up, my muscles burning, Robbie's hands fasten around my waist.

How can that feel so different to when Aleksi does it? Aleksi's hands are confident, precise. As another aerialist, he knows exactly how and where I need support.

Robbie's hands are fucking huge. He holds me like a dry leaf, his thumbs practically touching. I shudder again in his hold, and his eyes flick up to mine.

Something throbs hot, but it's not my wrist. My core clenches in on itself, aching to be filled.

I shake my head, banishing those thoughts from my mind. Focus.

With Aleksi's guidance and Robbie's hands taking my weight, I work through a series of static holds. I do a handstand on the bar, my pointed toes reaching for the ceiling. I hook one leg and hang upside down, spinning slowly. Under and over and around the bar, I move catlike, my skin glistening with sweat.

God. I've missed this so much.

These still holds aren't as fun as when the trapeze gets swinging, when I can soar and flip and twirl, but hanging from

54

this bar is home. Even with Robbie holding me up.

A whistle cuts through my hard breaths and Aleksi's murmurs. All three of our heads whip towards Kamran jogging towards the platform.

"What do you want, Lajani?" Robbie asks, his voice strained. I look at him properly for the first time since we started the holds. His pupils are blown wide, the blue of his eyes almost swallowed up by the black.

Huh.

A glance at Aleksi shows that his cheeks are dusted pink, too. I don't have time to sort through this new information, because Kamran leaps onto the stage.

He lands on the pads of his feet, barely making a noise. When he takes in the three of us together, Robbie's callused hands on my waist, his eyes glitter and his smile turns feral.

"Finally got Robbie's hands on you, eh, Hazel? How enviable."

Robbie plonks me down on the stage like a sack of potatoes. I stagger, huffing.

"There's potential," he grinds out at Aleksi, ignoring Kamran and me altogether. "See what you can do."

Then he's off, jumping onto the grass and striding out of the tent. I blink after him, watching the flush stain the back of his neck.

"Intriguing." I glance up at Kamran and he winks at me.

For once, I agree.

Chapter 6

On Monday night, I'm zipping into my stupid skeleton onesie when a low voice slides over me like honey. "Would you like help with that?"

Kamran pokes his head into the costume trailer, his amber eyes bright amid all that eyeliner. He cocks his head and smirks, glitter sparkling on his cheekbones.

I roll my eyes, adjusting the sleeves around my wrists. I took the liberty of chopping off those stupid mittens.

"I can dress myself, thanks."

Kamran's grin is shark-like. "Wonderful. You've finally figured out the buttons."

I grunt a laugh despite myself. The fire-eater has been teasing me more and more over the last few weeks, seeking me out each night at the fire pits. He's always smirking at me, whispering in my ear, or toying with a loose strand of my hair.

I...don't hate it, even when I bat him away. It makes my stomach flip.

"Oiled yourself up?" I let my eyes rake freely over his golden brown chest, his tight black pants, then fix them back on his face. He grins at me knowingly, and I want to punch him almost as much as I want to jump his bones.

There's such an ego on this guy. It's almost too bad that he's as gorgeous as he thinks.

"Yep. Oiled and ready." Kamran enters the trailer fully, brushing a finger along a costume rail. Sleeves in every color and style ripple under his touch. "It's only Monday, though. I thought I might sneak away."

I frown at the back of his head. Robbie has a zero tolerance policy for slacking. If Kamran skips work without a good excuse, he could get fired on the spot, no matter how long he's been here. It's not like we have contracts or a carnival HR department.

"Sneak where?"

Kamran shrugs, his body loose.

"The haunted house, perhaps."

I chew on my bottom lip, trying not to smile.

"It's more fun than I thought, I admit. Not worth Robbie's wrath, though."

Kamran glances over, a weird expression on his face. He looks almost tortured for a second, but then he blinks and it's gone.

"I'll take whatever parts of Robbie I can get," he says lightly, turning back to the make-up stand. A giant mirror surrounded by bulbs hangs on the wall above a counter. Lipsticks and face paints litter the counter, and black streaks of mascara dirty the glass. I watch Kamran's reflection grit his teeth, his agile fingers prodding at tubs of bronzer.

… Okay. There's a chance I've read this all wrong. I thought, with all his playful touches, all his whispered comments in my ear—

It doesn't matter. I shut it down, forcing my disappointment low in my gut. Crossing to Kamran's side, I nudge him with my elbow.

"Robbie with a fire-eater? He gets sunburn on cloudy days."

Kamran snorts, but when he catches my eye in the mirror, a frown steals over his face. He rounds on me, caging me against the wall of the counter, his arms blocking me in on both sides.

"Do you think I don't want you, Hazel?" His voice is rough, his eyes hard. "I want a man, so I can't want you too?"

I blink up at him, shaking my head. I haven't seen Kamran this serious since… well, ever.

"No," I force out, voice hoarse. "I don't think that."

Kamran nods once, hard, then seals his lips to my neck, sucking at the base of my jaw. He scrapes his teeth along my pulse point and I whimper.

Kamran grunts and crowds closer. He presses his body to mine, the evidence of just how much he wants me hard against my stomach.

I don't know what possesses me, but I grab a handful of his curls and whisper in his ear.

"Can you keep a secret?"

He wrenches his mouth away from my neck. "That depends who you ask."

I tug on his hair in warning. I'm trusting him with this, and though I must be mad, he'll come away worse off if he goes around telling my secrets.

"I want Robbie, too. And Aleksi."

Kamran groans and nips at my ear.

"Greedy girl. We'll get them aching for you."

* * *

Apparently Kamran truly doesn't give a shit, because he spends the evening's shift in the haunted house with me. He keeps his fire-eating costume on, not bothering to change, and he must run hot under that golden skin because it's an icy night.

At least it's not so frigid inside the ride. The rattling metal walls cut us off from the wind, and the whirring generators and warm bodies on the train warm up the air.

Still, Kamran and I stick close together. For temperature reasons.

Once again, he displays his knack for spooking the visitors riding the trains. He jumps out, screaming like he's gunning for an Oscar, his wild eyes unhinged. Kids and adults alike cower back in their seats, yelps drowning out the rattle of the train.

Kamran chuckles as he rejoins me in the shadows.

"I can see why you like this so much. What an ego trip."

"What are you implying, Lajani?"

He inches closer. "Nothing at all, darling."

It's been like this all night. Whatever happened in the costume trailer—it ratcheted the tension between us up to a new level. Every time the train moves out of sight, we grab for each other in the shadows and trade bruising, grasping kisses. I've sucked a love bite onto his collarbone; he bit down hard on my lip. There's no way we're walking out of here without the evidence written over our bodies, so I'm making the most of it.

Kamran starts talking again, no doubt teasing me about something, and I grab him by the belt loops.

"Save it for later." I jerk him against me, stifling a moan at the scorching heat of him pressed to my body. Even through the fleece of this stupid onesie, I can feel every dip and bulge of his muscled form.

Kamran laughs, delighted, and buries his hands in my hair.

The skeleton mask is somewhere on the floor, the hood pulled back. Any pretense of us working the ride is long gone.

"Shall we play a game?" Kamran asks as I lick a stripe up his throat. I hum against his smooth skin, breathing him in. He smells faintly of vanilla and jasmine, and I inhale another lungful.

"What kind of game?"

"You'll see in a moment."

I pull back, frowning. I've never liked surprises, and I especially don't want them from Kamran Lajani. He's the ultimate trickster; the carnival jester. He pickpockets the best of our thieves for fun; he starts fights just to soak in the chaos.

"What's going on?" I ask flatly, but heavy steps on the metal decking answers my question before Kamran can speak. Robbie ducks through the doorway, walking along the train ride tracks, his eyes moving straight towards us. We're wrapped around each other, lips swollen and hair wild. It couldn't be more obvious what we're doing back here if we put up a damn sign.

I shove Kamran off, fury blooming in my chest. Everything is a fucking game to him, and I'm a piece on the board, same as everyone else.

Kamran wants Robbie's attention? He lures him here, and coaxes me into the shadows. He kisses me, touches me like he means it, then throws it in Robbie's face.

I can't look at him. I can't look at either of them. I stare at my skeleton mask on the floor, pulse thundering in my ears.

"... Missed the show..." I hear Robbie say.

Kamran's reply is low, smoky. Something about inviting our stalwart boss to join.

I jerk my chin up and glare at Kamran, wishing I could

incinerate him with my eyes. When I speak, I can't keep the furious tremble from my voice, but at least I force out the words. I carve them out of the lump of hurt hardening in my chest.

"I wouldn't touch you again with a ten-foot pole. Fuck this. And fuck you, Lajani."

Robbie opens his mouth to say something—to yell at me too, probably—but I stomp past him and out the doorway. He can fire me later. Right now, my heart is pounding too hard, my spine damp with sweat. I'm humiliated, and anyone who's fool enough to stop me from leaving will get an earful.

No one tries.

The grounds are still open, the stalls selling, the rides running. There are visitors everywhere—smiling families, groups of drunken students—and everyone else is hard at work.

I can't go back to my trailer. Robbie or Kamran will know to find me there, and if I see either of them right now, I'll scream. I charge towards the big top tent instead, to where the lights are off and the crowd flows away.

Robbie never leaves until the show is done. Not with performers in the air. That means the tent has closed up for the night, and I can get some fucking peace.

My boot snags in a clump of grass, and I stumble, letting out a growl. It forms a tiny breath cloud, white against the night sky.

How could I be so stupid? First Yan, and now Kamran?

Cirque de la Lune is no place to let down your guard. To trust someone.

I go around the back of the tent. I don't want anyone's eyes on me, not even the stragglers from the audience. It's too much, too raw, and my head is still spinning with what Kamran has done.

Did I deserve that, somehow? Being used like that?

No. No way. I opened up, and he paid me back with lies and manipulation. Maybe he really wants me—the hard line of his cock pressed against my stomach implied that he does—but he still tossed it all aside for the chance to make Robbie jealous.

Tears burn in the back of my eyes; I blink them away. I won't cry over these assholes. Never again.

I duck through the slit in the canvas and let out a shuddering breath into the quiet. The tent is always eerie at night once everyone's gone. There's no wind, no roar of the crowd—only perfect stillness and the echoes of applause just on the edge of hearing.

"Hazel?"

Aleksi stares at me from behind the silks platform. He's bare-chested, a t-shirt held limply in his hands.

A shudder wracks through my chest, and I change course for him. Whatever scraps of sense I had, I left them with Kamran and Robbie. There's no voice now, telling me to stop. Only dark whispers urging me on.

I don't slow down as I reach him. I keep my pace until I slam into him, gripping his shoulders. Aleksi grunts as I shove him back against the platform, his t-shirt fluttering to the ground between us.

"Do you want this?" I ask, my breath sawing in and out. I must look fucking insane.

Aleksi swallows, his hands gentle on my elbows even as I dig my nails into his shoulders.

"Yes," he mutters, voice quiet. He sounds resigned, like he should know better.

He can join the fucking club.

I drop to the ground without another word, shoving his legs apart so I can kneel in between them. Aleksi inhales sharply as I tug at his pants, flicking the button open.

Before I reach inside, I sit back on my heels and meet his eyes.

"You're sure?"

I'm so wound up, my teeth are chattering. I could weep from relief when he nods.

"Yes."

His cock is thick and warm in my palm as I pull it free. It hardens under my grip, and when I stroke him from root to tip, Aleksi groans and becomes firmer than stone.

Fuck. Yes.

This is exactly what I need.

I lick and nibble up the length of him—a preliminary tease.

Then I swallow him down as far as I can, and I don't fucking hold back.

One of Aleksi's hands rests on my shoulder as I bob up and down; the other winds into my hair. He's gentle, always so fucking gentle, and I grip the hand fisted in my hair and urge him to hold on tighter. To tug, to use my mouth how he wants.

I want him to *take* me.

Aleksi is a quick learner. He steps closer, one palm on the back of my head holding me in place. I whimper with relief, resting both palms on his thighs as he fucks into my mouth. He's still careful, easing off when he hits the back of my throat, but his hands are firmer on me. They grip my jaw and hold me in place, and I work my tongue on him, swallowing hard.

Aleksi curses, his thigh muscles bunching under my palms, and begins to pull away. I lean forward, chasing him, taking him back into my throat until the tip of my nose brushes his stomach.

"God. God, Hazel."

Aleksi empties into my mouth, hot cum splashing my throat. I swallow it all, not pulling away until he's completely spent. When I finally ease back, jaw aching and throat sore, he's watching me with concern in his eyes.

It's too gentle again. Too much. I wipe my mouth on my sleeve and push to my feet.

"Don't tell anyone," I grit out, Kamran's little game still fresh in my mind.

Aleski hesitates, hurt flashing across his face, but he nods and steps back.

Good. Fine. That's taken care of.

I nod at him like a fucking weirdo and march back out of the tent. I need a better hiding spot. One without my ex's brother, with his broad chest and gentle eyes.

* * *

I can't slink out of the meeting by the fire pits. Robbie really would fire me then, and besides, I'd have to sneak right by everyone to get back to my trailer.

Better to get this bullshit over with.

Kamran and Robbie are already there, along with most of the workers. The bruise I sucked onto Kamran's collarbone is stark purple in the firelight, and already I can see people nudging each other and whispering.

You can't keep secrets in the carnival. No one can. And Kamran wears the bruise like a badge of honor, his eyes glittering as he watches me across the fire pits.

Whatever. I stare at the side of the nearest trailer, determined not to meet his gaze.

I charged off before Aleksi got his pants refastened, so at least we're not arriving together. Still, my hair is sex-wild and my make-up is probably smeared from the night's activities.

Kissing Kamran. Sucking off Aleksi. I'm a pissed off, busy bee. No doubt Kamran can read it all on my face, along with Robbie's all-knowing gaze.

Screw it. I look straight at the boss and find him watching me back. His expression is inscrutable as he takes in my rumpled hair, the grass stains on the knees of my costume, my angry, heaving chest. When his eyes flick up to mine again, a bolt of heat shoots through my core.

Fuck. Robbie looks at me like he wants to teach me a lesson.

Well, I've made enough epic mistakes for one night, so I swallow and look away. Ginny smiles at me cautiously from a rocking chair and I give her an awkward wave.

These people aren't idiots. They know exactly what I've been up to tonight. Whether they know it was with two separate guys is another question, but either way the rumor mill will be in full force before the meeting's up.

Everyone knows everyone's business here. Case in point: half these fuckers knew about Sasha and Yan before I did.

"Quiet one again," Robbie begins. "But it's Monday. To be expected."

He rattles through the highlights of the night—footfall, approximate takings. This is the only carnival I've worked at, but I have a feeling it's pretty rare for a boss to be so transparent. For everyone to know the ins and outs of the business, the boom months and the leaner times.

Robbie is straightforward. What you see is what you get.

Basically, he's the opposite of Kamran.

"Remember to do the job you're assigned." Robbie's eyes flick over me then dart to Kamran. Everyone must know what he's talking about—Kamran taking a night off from fire-eating to come make out with me in the haunted house. I stare into the nearest fire pit while everyone whispers to each other, watching the embers crackle and fly. "If you truly are surplus to requirements, then there's no need for you to stay."

That's got to be another dig at me. At my slow, shitty recovery. I'm not the one who dropped another performer, but I'm the one who's lagging now.

Surplus to requirements.

The fire pops loudly, and I inhale the smoke. This fucking night. The adrenalin that had me bursting out my skin earlier has drained away, leaving me sluggish. A kernel of a migraine throbs behind my right eye, and I screw it shut and dig in with the heel of my palm.

Robbie clips out a few more orders. Gives some terse updates. Then we're dismissed, free to drink or play cards or sleep or fuck until the morning. Chairs squeak as people push to their feet, slapping backs and stepping around each other.

I stand there, rooted to the spot, suddenly numb with exhaustion, and mentally run through my options.

There's my trailer. Tossing and turning in my bed, alone and angry.

There's Robbie and whatever lecture he has prepared. Kamran's silky excuses; Aleksi's gentle eyes.

Or there's alcohol. I spin on my heel, ready to drink myself into a stupor.

"Hazel!"

Danika jerks her chin at me from the next fire pit over. She's sat with the roadies again, all in faded black, a handful of cards clutched to her chest.

"Come play a few rounds."

My battered heart squeezes in my chest. I've been nothing but a brat to her, but Danika is planting a flag in the ground. Making a public statement of allegiance. I give my roomie a wobbly smile and drop into the empty seat next to her.

"What are we playing?"

They finish up the round, shuffling the deck back together. When a bearded man with a tattooed neck and an earring deals us all in, he gives me a slight smile.

I don't even know these guys. Crap. What's his name?

"Derek," he mutters, like he heard my thoughts. "This is Jackson, Andrea, GJ, and Zack."

I nod at the other roadies, trying to mentally pin names to faces. The roadies tend to be a few years older than the performers—in their thirties rather than their twenties. Looking at Danika now, she seems older than I first thought, too. I haven't even tried to get to know her.

Goddamn it. I'm the worst.

I settle back into my chair, ready to make up for lost time. Danika won my undying loyalty the second she went out on a limb for me like that.

"I suck at cards," I announce to the group. "Don't hold back. Give me a proper thrashing."

"Don't let Robbie hear you say that," Derek says, but he's grinning. "I'm sure the boss would be all too happy to oblige."

I stick my tongue out at him and start ordering my cards.

Teasing, I can handle. I've made a spectacle of myself, after all. It'd be worse if they tip-toed around me—then I'd know I should really be ashamed.

It turns out the roadies are really fucking fun. Without the pressure of performing, of having to compete for the best spots, there's a hell of a lot less ego kicking around this group. They're just a bunch of people who looked at the normal path through life—the career, the spouse, the mortgage—and decided, no thanks. Or at least, not yet.

They ran away with the circus, and they're living the dream. They work hard and play hard, all under the glow of the stars.

They figured out what they wanted, and they took it. When I picture my life beyond the trapeze, I see...

Nothing.

I see nothing. Just blank space.

I have no damn idea who I am when my feet are back on the ground.

Chapter 7

Aleksi is all business the next morning at our training session. He hands me a bottle of water without a word when I arrive, gesturing for me to warm up. My muscles are already loose and limber from my workout before breakfast, but I do what I'm told.

I don't like the pinch to Aleksi's mouth, or the shadows under his eyes.

"Have a good night?"

I cringe at my awkwardness, bending over one knee in the splits. One hand stretches over my head to grip my ankle bone, and I sigh at the pop in my back.

I've been so damn stiff lately. All tensed up and on edge.

Aleksi doesn't even look at me. He inspects the trapeze like he does every session, checking and rechecking the structure. I don't bother checking for myself anymore when I step up to the bar. Aleksi is so thorough he's verging on OCD, and I trust him to keep me in one piece.

Ironic really, considering his brother is the one who hurt me in the first place.

I try again. "How did the show go?"

"Fine." His words are clipped. "It's always fine."

That's true enough—Aleksi is as picky and exacting with his

own standards as he is with mine. Every night, he delivers a flawless performance to a gasping crowd. People come from miles around to watch Aleksi on the silks; he even has a few hardcore fans who visit us in every town.

It's a wonder his ego isn't bigger.

"Do anything fun after?" I ask, then screw my eyes shut. I sit up straight and fight the urge to stuff my whole fist in my mouth. I meant playing cards, or drinking with the musicians, or letting the fortune tellers read his palm.

Not pulling my hair while I sucked him off twenty feet from here.

Aleksi levels me a look.

"Stretch your wrist out, Hazel."

I clam up and work through my stretches. Fine. Forget making conversation. If Aleksi wants to be weird about this, that's on him.

I'm dusting my hands with chalk when he finally speaks up.

"I didn't tell anyone. Like you said." He frowns at the trapeze bar like it's offended him. "Everyone probably thought it was Kamran who made you so... rumpled."

Yeah. I grimace, already sweating through the chalk. But he deserves to know, so I force the words through my teeth.

"It sort of was Kamran. As well as you, I mean. He ditched the show to work in the haunted house last night."

Not that we did much working, but I don't spell that part out. Aleksi's eyes narrow, and that blush is back on his cheeks.

He gets it.

And I feel about three inches tall when he rakes a hand through his hair, face bewildered.

"Why did you come to me, then?"

He sounds so hurt. Fuck. I haven't had nearly enough coffee

for this conversation, but I clear my throat and try to look him in the eye.

"Because I like you. Um. Both of you." Aleksi opens his mouth to say something, but I push on. There's no way I'm building up to this twice. "Maybe Robbie too, for the record. Not that any of it matters, because Robbie's repressed and Kamran's a prick, and you're clearly not the type to share. But… still. I guess you should know."

There's a long stretch when he says nothing and I pick at a scratch on the trapeze bar.

"Anyone else?" he asks at last, voice hoarse.

I shake my head.

Aleksi clears his throat and taps the back of my hand.

"Come on, then. Before your muscles go cold."

He doesn't mention last night's shit show again, but the dark shadows beneath his eyes seem to fade a little. A few times, when I clown around, squawking for help, his mouth twitches into a smile. Each time, I feel like punching the air.

It's a win. I'll take it.

My wrist aches, but it can hold part of my weight, and it's less stiff when I stretch it out before training. Aleksi still braces me, his hands firm on my waist, but it's progress, and I'm drenched in sweat by the end.

I snort when I catch him wiping his hands on his jeans. My vest top is soaked through, and he's been holding me up like a trooper.

"What did you do to piss Robbie off so much that he gave you this job?"

I've been chewing it over privately and coming up with nothing. It's not like Aleksi doesn't have better things to do. He could be working out, choreographing routines, checking his equipment—hell, he could nap. Aleksi's an athlete, so sleep is gold dust to him.

He frowns at me like he's confused.

"I volunteered. I offered to do it."

Shit. Living in Cirque de la Lune long term hardens you up. I'm so used to seeing people with all their rough edges on show—drinking, fighting, gambling. I live with pickpockets and arsonists. And even though I've had no real trouble, I keep a baseball bat under my bed.

I forget there are people who are just good. Straightforward and kind. Aleksi hasn't lost that living here; I just wasn't looking for it.

I swallow around the knot in my throat. When I smile at him, my chin wobbles.

"You're a good guy, Aleksi."

His eyebrows go up in surprise, and when his mouth quirks up, it's like the sun came out.

I can't help myself. I drag my sweaty body over to him and press my lips to his. After a moment, his arms wind around me, never mind how gross I am, and we lock together, breathing each other in.

I could stay like this forever.

Except I really stink.

"See you later," I say, stepping out from his arms, suddenly shy. I hop down to the grass and take off before I change my mind.

Shower. Then panic about kissing my ex's brother. But first, shower.

* * *

"I may have miscalculated."

Sadly, I can't avoid Kamran forever. I pointedly sit on the other side of the fire pits, and leave the costume trailer or food trucks whenever he walks in, but he still corners me eventually. I'm on the roof of a truck with Danika, swigging beers. It's a Saturday night, which translates to a long fucking night.

I'm cold, even bundled in two sweaters, and my muscles are aching.

"So you have," I tell the head that's popped up between our legs. "Wrong truck, asshole."

Kamran's face sours, but he still pulls himself over the lip of the roof. I huff as we're forced to make room for him, his wide shoulders pushing between us.

"You can't run from me forever, Hazelnut. Let me explain." His elbow catches me in the boob and I grunt, shoving him off.

"I'd rather not."

Danika's voice is thick with amusement as she shuffles to the edge of the truck.

"I think I'll go find a game somewhere." She turns back and winks. "Good luck, Kamran."

"Don't encourage him!" I yell after her as she drops to the ground. Kamran reaches over to pass her beer bottle, and they murmur something to each other.

For God's sake. I shuffle to the edge, too, ready to go find Aleksi or Ginny.

"Oh, no you don't."

Kamran rests a palm on my leg. He's not gripping hard, but for some stupid reason, I pause. I glare at him, my jaw clenched and my chest heaving under my sweatshirts. I hate how much he affects me, even now.

He used me. Paraded me in front of Robbie like a dog at a

73

show.

"I suppose you've already texted Robbie? What shall I do, straddle your lap?"

Kamran sighs, rubbing a hand down his face. It smears his eyeliner and glitter together.

"I deserve that."

"No shit." I wriggle towards the edge again. Whatever his excuse is, I don't want to hear it.

I'd never use another person like that. Messing with their feelings for show. Never.

Kamran grabs a fistful of my sweatshirt, holding me loosely. I could shake him off if I tried, but instead I fling out a hand to flip him off.

"Oof."

My finger connects with something squishy. I turn back and find Kamran grimacing, one hand clapped over his eye.

"Shit. Sorry. Are you okay?"

He mutters something, rubbing at his eye socket. I spin onto my knees, crawling closer, trying to get a look.

"Is it scratched?"

I nudge my knee between his legs, pulling at his wrists to show me the damage. Kamran ducks his head, mumbling under his breath, until I'm stretched over him, wrestling the bastard.

Suddenly, he pulls his hand away, throwing me off balance. I fall forward into him, my chin against his chest, and we topple back onto the truck roof. The metal clangs, loud enough for the fire pits to hear, and wolf whistles float over on the night air.

"Fucker."

I smack at his ribs where they're shaking with laughter. He's stretched out, long and lean beneath me, and I taste his smoke and spice scent on my tongue.

An ache throbs between my thighs, and I roll off to one side. It doesn't matter how good Kamran feels under me. He's still a manipulative prick.

"You can't resist, can you? Everything is a trick."

I sit up and gather my knees, resting my chin on the denim of my jeans. Out of the corner of my eye, I see Kamran rock upright and settle at my side.

We both stare out at the carnival grounds. The lights, the smoke, the stars.

"There's a tiny cut on my cheek, actually."

I glance over. A little red crescent marks his perfect cheekbone.

I grunt. "Maybe Robbie likes scars."

Kamran shifts closer, his warmth seeping through my clothes. All that fire he eats must simmer away in his gut.

"I'm sorry," Kamran says, and it's so unexpected coming from him that I shake my head to clear it. "I thought we understood each other. That we both wanted him jealous."

I chew that over, watching the shadow of a fox sniffing around the hot dog stand. It presses its nose to the grease-coated walls, scrabbling a paw at the doorway.

"I don't want to be a means to an end."

"You're not." Kamran sounds pissed off. "You never would be."

A reluctant smile twists my lips, and I nudge him with my shoulder.

"It would be pretty hot with Robbie."

Kamran sighs. "The three of us would start forest fires."

He says it so tragically that I burst out laughing, my voice ringing through the night air. He chuckles with me, inching closer until he's sealed to my side.

"I sucked Aleksi off," I tell him casually. Best to get it all out in the open.

Kamran hums. "I bet that was a sight."

"Do you like him too?" I ask, genuinely curious. Kamran stalls before answering, flopping back to lie with his arms crossed under his head.

"No," he says finally, staring straight up. "Just Robbie. And you. You most of all."

It sounds kind of ridiculous, to be fiercely committed to two people that you're not even with.

I get it, though. More and more each day, there are only three faces I see when I close my eyes.

The trickster.

The acrobat.

And the man in charge of it all.

Even pressed together as we are, Kamran doesn't try anything, and neither do I. I've been burned, and I need to lick these wounds a while longer.

Besides, I trusted Yan with my life—and look where that got me. My wrist throbs, as if in agreement, and I burrow deeper into my sweater.

It doesn't matter if I have a few stupid crushes. If I can't perform again, there's no room for me in Cirque de la Lune.

* * *

I barge back into our trailer right as Danika pulls her shirt over her head. Inked across her ribs and back in vivid jewel tones are a mermaid, an anchor, an octopus. They tangle around

76

each other, along with other symbols of the seabed: a treasure chest, an oyster displaying its pearls, a shoal of tiny fish.

"Holy shit."

Danika jerks her top back down, her cheeks flaming. Her short curls are rumpled by the almost-change, and the irritated glance she sends me is like day one all over again.

"Danika." I close the trailer door behind me, shutting in the cozy glow from our lamps. "That tattoo is the shit."

She presses her lips together, gesturing for me to turn my back while she changes. I spin and kick off my boots while she rustles behind me.

"I'm serious," I tell the floor. "Why are you hiding it? That's the best ink in this whole damn circus."

"I'm not hiding it. It's November," she says dryly. "Not bikini season."

Still, the irritation is gone when I turn back around. A smile tugs at the corner of her mouth, and she sits cross-legged on her bed, watching me shove down my leggings. I've lived in the circus for years now, and any body-shyness got drilled out of me ages ago. You can't be prudish when you're onstage in nothing but a leotard, the spotlights picking out your every flaw.

"Yours are cool, too."

I grin at Danika, sticking out a bare leg. Dark roses creep up my thigh, with bird skulls and berries and white masks hidden in their foliage.

Mom and Dad had a fit when they saw my first ever tattoo. Even now, when I visit home, their faces tinge green at the sight.

"What did Kamran want?" Danika asks at last, voice sly. I roll my eyes, flopping back on my mattress.

"What doesn't he want?" I mumble at the ceiling. There's a crack, splintering from the corner of the trailer right over my bed.

"At least he's up front with it."

I hum, nibbling my thumb nail. No one could ever accuse Kamran of being coy.

It's ironic, really. The biggest trickster in the circus, and he's the most straightforward guy I've ever met.

* * *

Two nights later, Ginny is woozy so I pack up her hot dog stall. I scrub down the surfaces and load all the ingredients into cold storage, wrinkling my nose at the stink of oil. Damn, this stuff tastes good, but behind the scenes it's a wreck. There's such a thick coat of grease on everything that I scrub until my shoulder burns, and I've still barely cut through to the metal beneath.

Next time I'm hungry, I'm hitting up the popcorn stand.

Fighting a losing battle with the grease makes me flushed and sweaty, and I slide my skeleton onesie off my shoulders and tie the sleeves at my waist. The frigid night air pricks my bare arms like needles, my nipples pebbling under my vest.

Pausing after half an hour, I sniff the fabric of my top.

I stink like week-old hot dogs. Perfect.

"No company tonight? Where are your boy toys?"

I whip my head around, my ponytail lashing my face. The other food stands packed up already, and this part of the carnival grounds is shadowed and empty. A burly guy leans against the next stall over, his tattooed arms crossed over his chest.

He's in worn jeans and a leather jacket. He works the air rifles, maybe, or a ride.

I don't like the look in his eyes. Like he's cornered me. Like I'm prey.

"Actually, they just ran to get something," I lie, my heart speeding up in my chest. "They'll be back any second."

I know guys like this, and lashing out about his boy toy comment is the last thing I need to do. What I need is to put several hundred feet between me and that glint in his eyes.

The man grunts. He's vaguely familiar, with his dark beard and buzzed head, but I don't know his name. Can't place where I've seen him before. I wrack my brain, in case acting like I know him will make him think twice about whatever bad idea he's had.

"How are the… trucks?" I hazard, racing to lock up Ginny's stall with fumbling hands. She can handle a little leftover grease. I need to get out here.

The guy snorts. "Nice try. You don't give a shit who I am."

Not true. I may not have noticed him before, but I definitely give a shit now. For starters, I'm about to sprint to Robbie and demand this psycho gets kicked out.

"Your boys aren't coming, either," he breathes.

Fuck. I drop the padlock and run.

I lunge around the side of the stall and race across the grass. It's dark here, but there's a floodlight up ahead, and if I can just get visible, if they can see me from the fire pits—

A massive weight slams into my back and smashes me into the ground. I tuck my wrists into my chest out of instinct, then slam face-first into the dirt. Grass and mud fill my eyes, my mouth, and I'm screaming through the weeds. I throw back my elbows, thrashing under the man's weight, but he's three times my size. He wrestles my wrists together with practiced hands.

"Come on, slut," he grunts, his breathing heavy. He clamps down on my wrists with one big hand while the other tugs at the back of my onesie. I scream and buck harder. "We all know you want it."

I wrench one arm free and punch back blindly, aiming for his crotch. There's an *oof*, and then his weight disappears from my back. I surge to my feet, spinning around with my hands raised.

Robbie stands over the guy, holding him up by the shirt while he punches him in the face. Again and again, his fist slams into the guy's face, blood splattering from the broken nose. The man's eyes swell up and his chin grows wet with spit, and still Robbie beats him into the dirt.

At first glance, Robbie looks weirdly calm, his features smooth. Then I prod my injured wrist and suck in a breath at the pain, and Robbie glances over with wild eyes.

He drops the guy in the dirt and steps over him, crossing to my side. His battered hand shakes as he cups my wrist gently, turning it in his palms.

"Did he hurt you?"

His voice is hard, but his fingers are so fucking careful. I shake my head, my throat tight.

Cuts and bruises, yes. A throbbing wrist, yes.

But not the way he wanted.

"Come on."

Robbie drops my wrist and walks back to the guy. Without warning, he draws his boot back and kicks him square in the crotch. The guy screams, his voice breaking, curling his knees to his chest.

When Robbie speaks, his voice is low, but it's so empty here that I catch his words.

"I see your face again and you die. Clear out and start running."

He ignores the gasping, sobbing wreck at his feet and turns back to me. His palm trembles where he places it on my back and guides me across the grounds to his trailer.

"Great, more rumors," I joke lamely, not sure what else to say. This entire night is surreal, unhinged from reality, and I'm dizzy from that sick rush of fear. "Now they'll all think I'm after three men."

Robbie says nothing, just leads me past the fire pits. Curious faces watch us go; Aleksi and Kamran stand up, frowning.

I duck my head, following Robbie. I don't want them to see me like this.

"In," Robbie says, holding his trailer door open. Our audience's eyes burn into my back as I walk up the squeaky metal steps.

The door closes behind him, and Robbie flicks on the light. It's quiet in here, and surprisingly tidy. There's a double bed pushed into the corner, with gray sheets tucked in military-style. Nearby is a bookshelf and a desk, everything fastened down or tucked away so it doesn't slide everywhere when we drive. A sofa bench lines one wall, with a small table in front of it, and a bathroom door is slightly ajar, the shower visible inside.

I don't know what I expected. Something more decadent, maybe? Robbie is in charge, at the top of the heap, but his trailer looks like anyone else's.

"Sit."

I lower myself onto the sofa bench. Guess we've regressed

81

to one-word commands.

"Look, I'm sorry," I say, but Robbie sucks in a breath, nostrils flaring.

"Don't you dare. That piece of shit should never have been working here."

He digs a first aid kit out of a cupboard and kneels between my legs. I watch him, heart hammering, as he inspects the cuts and grazes on my arms and my face.

There's a tiny scar through one of his eyebrows. And he smells like cut grass and wood smoke. I guess I'm still checked out of my mind, because I lean forward and breathe him in freely. I stare at him like I'm cataloguing his features, like I'll never get this close again and I need to savor it.

"Sit back," he tells me, voice strained. I do as he says, but my thighs tighten around him. "Hazel..."

Something about that warning note in his voice makes me shift restlessly on the bench. I look up instead, counting marks on the ceiling instead of focusing on the slide of his fingers over my skin.

He cleans every single cut and graze, even the tiny ones. I hiss with each swipe of antiseptic fluid, and his mouth twists at the sound.

Robbie doesn't stop, though. Not until I'm patched up like the world's wimpiest soldier. He runs his eyes over me one last time then goes to stand, but I catch his forearm.

"Your turn."

I tug his right hand into my lap. The knuckles are cracked and swollen, covered in that other man's blood. Ignoring Robbie's laser stare, I rummage in the first aid kit and set to work. I wipe off all the blood and disinfect his entire hand, then bandage up the worst cuts.

Robbie doesn't hiss like me. He barely even breathes. He kneels there, turned to stone, while I try my best to patch him up.

I sit back once I'm done, his hand still held in mine. The silence stretches out, and I wait for him to say something. Anything.

"Go back to your trailer. You can skip the meeting tonight."

Okay, maybe not anything. I gape up at him as he stands and walks out without another word.

My cuts sting, and my body aches from slamming into the ground. I'm stiff when I stand and inch my way to the door.

My trailer it is. I'm ready for tonight to be a memory.

Chapter 8

I skip my workout the next morning, on account of how my body feels like it's been hit by a grand piano. I sit with Danika at breakfast, studiously ignoring the whispers and less-than-stealthy questions about my night.

They'll all hear about it one way or another. There are no secrets at the carnival. But that doesn't mean I owe them all the gory details.

Kamran comes over, but he's surprisingly restrained about it. He just hands me a steaming mug of coffee and starts chatting about some kid who got so excited by the fire-eaters that he pissed himself last night.

I take a sip, stifling a moan at the hot, creamy goodness. Loads of milk, no sugar. Exactly how I like it.

I have no idea how Kamran takes his coffee, but I resolve to find out.

By the time I arrive at the big top tent to train with Aleksi, my muscles are loosening up. I've been tense since I heard that guy's voice outside Ginny's stall, and I spooked at every little noise outside my trailer last night. But the bright sunshine and the people all around are slowly reassuring my rabbit brain that I'm safe.

"What happened?"

Aleksi cuts straight to the point. He hasn't even set up for the session. He's pacing in front of the platform, glowering at the grass. He stops when he sees me coming, shoving his hands on his hips.

He looks about as tense as I am.

"Just some asshole out by the food stalls." I fight to keep my voice light. "We dealt with him. It doesn't matter now."

"Doesn't matter?" Aleksi pinches the bridge of his nose. He looks like steam should flow out of his ears. "What the hell is that supposed to mean?"

I toss my water bottle onto the stage and tug my sweatshirt over my head.

"It means I don't want to talk about it."

Aleksi barks out a laugh. "Right. God forbid we talk."

I frown, my shoulders creeping up around my ears again. "I don't know what you're saying, Aleksi."

"I mean sure, you can suck me off then pretend nothing ever happened, but talking about something like a grown ass adult—"

"He attacked me! What the fuck do you want me to say?"

I blink at him, stomach lurching and hands held wide, then feel my face crumple. Aleksi's there before I can move, his muscular arms winding around me and holding me tight to his chest. His palm strokes up and down my back as I sob into his sweater. My nose is definitely running too, but if I leave a snot trail, that is all his fault.

I sniff and thump him on the shoulder.

"Asshole. Told you I didn't want to talk."

He nods, his chin ruffling my hair.

"Don't tell Yan," I whisper into the wool. Aleksi stiffens, but nods again.

I don't care how close he is with his brother. My life stopped being Yan's business the second he walked away without a backwards glance.

The reminder of who we have in common is enough to drive us apart. We step away awkwardly; me dabbing at my face with my sleeve, and Aleksi surreptitiously wiping the snot off his sweater.

He clears his throat.

"Are you all right to train?"

I roll my neck. "Definitely."

I woke up with a new fire in my belly. If I'd landed differently when that prick tackled me last night—if even worse things had happened—I could have been off the trapeze for months longer. My career could have been over.

Life is short, and there are no guarantees.

I need to get back in the air.

* * *

It doesn't take much wheedling to get the trapeze set higher. I want to swing, to start proper aerial work, and Aleksi understands that better than anyone. He looks more at home fifty feet in the air than he does with both feet on the ground.

"Go easy to begin with," he tells me, stern. "Build up from there."

I nod along, only half listening. It's been months. I'm so freaking excited.

He still makes me wear the safety harness, and for once I don't grumble about it. We're not just practicing holds a few feet off the ground anymore. I'm about to fly.

It's still not as high as during a show, and without a partner there's only so much I can do. Yan taught me everything I know, so there was no need for him to teach me the solo stuff.

I was there to make him look good. I get that now.

Even though Aleksi and Yan look so damn similar—same brown eyes, square jaw, left cheek dimple—they couldn't be more different in their teaching style. Yan was all about the partner work; Aleksi is pushing me to go solo. Yan would get distracted and chatter about everything; Aleksi is silent and stern.

Yan used to touch me at every opportunity, kissing me against every available surface.

Aleksi doesn't touch me for the whole session, even when the proximity leaves me hot and aching, my skin singing out for his touch. I'm about ten seconds from tugging my shirt over my head and draping myself over the nearest speaker when Kamran sidles in, a smirk curling his lips.

He whistles. "Looking good, Hazelnut."

I soar overhead, shooting him a grin. I'm only doing the most basic moves, and I have to stop every ten minutes to rest my wrist.

It still feels so fucking good. I don't know how I made it for months without this.

By the time my feet are back on the ground, Kamran and Aleksi stand side by side. They've been watching me, murmuring together, heads bent close.

If I thought Kamran liked Aleksi too, I might have felt a flicker of jealousy. Instead, hunger clenches in my core as I sidle over to both of them. Successfully working the trapeze on my own has made me cocky, and I give my hips a little extra sway.

They both notice. I watch their eyes darken in the same

breath. But where Kamran grins at me, his face filled with promise, Aleksi turns away. He grabs his bag of training kit and swings it onto his shoulder.

"I'll leave you both to it."

He won't meet my eyes, and my heart speeds up for a different reason. This feels like a crossroads, like a test, and I glance at Kamran before I step forward.

Kamran gives me a tiny nod.

Screw it. You don't try; you don't get.

"Wait." I grab Aleksi's sleeve, tugging him to a stop. He finally looks at me then, hurt flickering deep in his eyes. "Don't go," I murmur. "I don't want you to go. Please."

Aleksi glances at Kamran, who smirks back.

He opens his mouth, but no words come out.

"Why don't we go find some coffee," Kamran offers. He's so good at stuff like this—smoothing over other people's rough edges. He's like the molten gold that seals together the edges of those famous broken vases.

I watch Aleksi, chewing on my bottom lip.

"All right," he rasps after a moment. "Coffee. Yeah."

I get the mad urge to whoop and jump into the air, but I tamp that shit down. No way am I going to scare him off now. Not when we're so close, inching towards the precipice of something... incredible.

These two together make me feel like I'm soaring on that trapeze. Wild and untethered. *Free.*

A traitorous voice in my mind whispers Robbie's name, but I ignore that too. No point pining after something that will never happen. Robbie has barely said three nice sentences to me since I came back, and he's my boss.

Even if by some miracle he was still interested after all that,

Robbie is not the sort of man to share.

"Let's go." I slide my hand into Aleksi's and grin when he grips me back. Kamran leads us across the tent, his musical voice chattering about nonsense.

Aleksi leans close, murmuring in my ear so only I can hear.

"I still want to get you alone, Hazel."

I shiver. That makes two of us.

* * *

Coffee turns out to just be coffee.

I don't know what I expected. A threesome right there at the food stalls?

Either way, this is probably better. Kamran, Aleksi and I just talk, chatting about nothing and everything. We take our cups to go, heading back to the fire pits and sitting around last night's ashes.

Danika winks at me when she walks past, and heat prickles across my cheeks. I know what they're all thinking. Hell, I'm hoping they're right.

If they're not, this is kind of awkward.

Kamran is a lot to get used to, all dramatic gestures and outright lies and shameless innuendo. He's not exactly the first person you'd match with quiet, steady Aleksi.

The acrobat takes it in stride, though. He keeps a firm hold on my hand all the way to the fire pit, ignoring the stares from the other workers, and he only lets go when we all drop into our lawn chairs.

He even gets Kamran talking about his family back home. That's something I've never managed myself—Kamran is slippery about personal details.

Turns out he has three little sisters.

I wonder if they wear half as much glitter as he does.

After the horror show of last night and the adrenalin spike of the trapeze this morning, I'm half asleep already and it's not even noon. The full day of fixing up stalls and working the haunted house stretches before me, and I stifle a yawn in my sleeve.

"You need stronger coffee," a voice says behind my chair.

I pause, not turning around.

I'm not doing anything wrong, hanging out with these guys. We're friends, regardless of anything else, and it's no one's business if we want to be more.

So why does guilt curdle in my gut?

"Hey," I mutter to Robbie. He circles my chair to face me, raking his eyes over my body like he might have missed something last night.

Kamran slides an inch lower in his chair, suddenly absorbed in rubbing a stain off his coffee mug. Aleksi glances between Kamran and Robbie with a frown creasing his forehead.

Yeah. This whole setup is kind of a mess.

"How's the wrist?" Robbie asks.

Of course that's what he's after. Can I still train, am I ready to get back to work?

I press my lips together. "Fine."

His eyes narrow, but he doesn't push.

"Hazel's taking her full weight now," Aleksi supplies. He's not usually the chatty type, but I guess he's taking pity on me. "She'll be doing full routines soon."

"Good." Robbie jerks his chin. Then, to me: "Time to look for a partner."

My heart sinks all the way from my chest to the base of my

stomach. Aleksi has been pushing so hard for me to go solo, I figured Robbie must be on board. I thought he was, that other time in training…

"Sure." I force a smile. "On it, boss."

I wait until his back is turned and he's striding away to deflate. Kamran mutters to himself as I tap at my mug, not wanting to meet anyone's eyes.

I don't want to see the pity there. It makes everything so much worse.

"I'll talk to him," Aleksi offers, and I can't keep the snap from my voice.

"Leave it. If Robbie says I need a partner, then I need a partner."

Closing my eyes, I rest my head back on the chair with a thunk. We can't all be Aleksi Genkov, star performer of every show.

* * *

I decide a nap is on the cards after all, drifting away from the fire pits after lunch. After a few steps, I notice Aleksi keeping stride, but I don't send him away.

It's not his fault I haven't impressed Robbie. Without Aleksi, I'd still be squeezing my stress ball and wondering when I'd get in the air.

"He's an idiot."

I snort. I don't think I've ever heard Aleksi call someone out. Still, there's a reason Cirque de la Lune is one of the biggest carnivals in the country. Robbie is no one's fool.

"Hardly."

We fall back into silence, our strides eating up the ground.

It's one of those bright November mornings where the sun shines fierce but it's not enough to burn away the cold. The trees lining the edge of the clearing are balding, their brown leaves snatched away on the wind.

"He really screwed me," I mutter at the grass, and we both know I'm not talking about Robbie. Aleksi glares at the dirt too, his mouth twisted to one side.

He and Yan were inseparable before he left. I used to tease Aleksi that he was the third in our relationship, laughing when his cheeks turned pink. I don't know what Aleksi thinks of Yan leaving, but I know he's loyal to a fault.

He won't speak against his brother, no matter what state he left me in.

"You don't need Yan," he offers instead.

It's not enough.

My chest feels hollow as I push my trailer door open. Aleksi follows behind, wiping his boots on the mat. I don't want to talk—my mouth is glued shut—but I don't want to be alone either. Not curled up on the bed I used to share with Yan most nights, my arms hugging my own rib cage.

Aleksi pauses behind me, the warmth of his body spreading over my back. The trailer is silent apart from our breathing as he draws my hair over one shoulder.

His lips press to the bare skin of my neck, right at the knob of my spine. My eyes drift closed and I breathe in through my nose, my throat suddenly tight.

"You're tense again."

Aleksi drags his lips around the side of my neck to the spot below my ear. He steps closer, too, and I sway back until I'm leaning against his chest.

"Wouldn't you be?"

He hums, the vibration skittering over my skin.

One hand drags up the length of my arm, pausing to knead my shoulder. I tilt my head with a groan, biting my lip at the sensation—equal parts pain and relief.

Aleksi and I know all about that. Waiting, secretly wanting, then the relief that feels almost too much. Another hand grips my hip hard and grinds us closer together.

Yeah. This has been a long time coming between us. Even before Yan left, it felt inevitable somehow.

"Tell me to stop," Aleksi orders me.

I turn in his arms. "Not a chance."

Our mouths slam together, all those months and years of private longing pouring out where our lips meet. It's bruising and angry, a battle for dominance, teeth nipping hard.

"Do you still want to keep this a secret?" Aleksi asks between snatched breaths. We stumble towards my unmade bed, tripping over each other's feet.

It's a bit late for secrets, after he held my hand all morning. And besides—I'm done hiding.

I yank a fistful of his t-shirt, hard.

"Screw that. Make me scream."

We topple onto the mattress in a chorus of springs, wrestling each other to be on top. Aleksi's stronger, obviously, and he lays me down easily, my heart pounding and my pussy aching in my leggings. I wrap my legs around his waist, squeezing him hard just to prove a point.

"Stop wriggling."

He tugs my leggings and panties down in one motion. I'm bare to him, the cool November air on my pussy, and I pull my knees up to urge him on.

Aleksi stares between my legs, two spots of color glowing

high on his cheekbones. I've seen that look on his face before—many times, over the years. When Yan grabbed me and kissed me in the food line, or when my skin was slick with sweat after a show.

"Worth the wait?" I ask. It's meant to be teasing, but it comes out unsure.

Aleksi glares at me, brown eyes fierce.

"Worth waiting forever."

I'm about to make another lame joke—something about not even touching it yet—when Aleksi slides down the bed and buries his face between my thighs. He licks hard up my slit, flattening his tongue against my core. I fist my hands in his hair, forgetting to breathe, and jam my head against the pillow.

"Fuck. Aleksi. Fuck."

He eats me out like I'm the best thing he's ever tasted. He's decadent with it, exploring every inch of me with the tip of his tongue, suckling on my folds. When my oxygen-starved brain finally remembers to take a breath, he thrusts his tongue deep inside me.

"Shit!"

My hips raise off the bed, and he pushes me back down with his forearm, plunging his tongue deeper. Aleksi is merciless, alternating between licking into my pussy and sliding his fingers inside while he laps at my clit. I lose my fucking mind, babbling nonsense worthy of Kamran at the ceiling until tears well in my eyes.

The pressure builds with every lick, every stroke. His fingers crook inside me, rubbing against my walls.

"Fuck!"

My thighs clamp down on his head, and I come apart with a cry. It's messy and uncoordinated, my muscles spasming as I clench around his fingers. Aleksi licks me through it all, pushing me higher and higher until I finally have to shove him away, oversensitive.

"Fuck," I say again, falling back against the pillows. My ears are ringing. Aleksi drags himself up to lie alongside me, the whole lower half of his face wet and shining.

"Here." I pull up a corner of the blanket and dab at his face. He snorts and I break into giggles, suddenly giddy.

Footsteps on the trailer stairs have Aleksi yanking the blanket to cover me. We scramble upright as Danika nods at us, a smirk tugging the corner of her mouth.

"Oh, Aleksi." She spins around on the way to her bed. "Someone was just looking for you. A guy called Yan?"

My giddy heart plummets through the trailer floor and six feet into the soil.

Chapter 9

The last time I saw Yan, I was bundled into Ginny's car to go to the hospital. My wrist was swollen, clumsily bound in one of the roadie's flannel shirts and clutched against my chest.

Yan stood beside the passenger window, his mouth tipped down in a sorrowful frown.

"Get well soon, Hazel," he called, like he wasn't the asshole that dropped me.

And all that time, his arm was around Sasha.

Needless to say, seeing Yan again is not on my bucket list. There is zero guarantee that a red haze won't come over my vision and I'll wake up covered in man blood.

Aleksi, on the other hand, can't get out there fast enough. He smooths his clothes down, scrubs at his face with his sleeve—tries to remove every trace of evidence. I watch him with my leggings pooled around my ankles, the blanket dragged up to my waist.

"Bye, then," I mutter as Aleksi crams his feet into his boots. He glances over at me, but barely.

"Bye."

His footsteps are heavy on the trailer steps, then his boots thud against the grass. Danika and I listen to him go, my gaze fixed on my knees.

When I finally look at her, she cocks her head.

"At least I got off this time," I joke weakly. Who am I kidding? I feel like shit. I'm about one more rejection away from Googling the nearest convent.

Danika just rolls her eyes.

"These idiots. I swear to God."

I'm not one hundred percent sure whether she's including me in that statement, but either way I'd have to agree. I knew full well that tumbling into bed with my ex-boyfriend's brother would be a mess, and I did it anyway.

At least I came so hard I saw stars. You've got to find the silver lining.

"Is Yan out there now?"

Danika shakes her head, so I shimmy my leggings back up under the blanket. I stuff my shoes back in my boots and throw on a thicker sweatshirt, ready to go and bitch to Kamran.

When I hop down the trailer steps, though, Yan waves at me from the fire pits, calling out to me so everyone hears.

"Son of a..."

I grumble under my breath as I cross the open field. If I flip him off like I want to, I'll look petty—or even worse, like I care. I smooth my features as I near the fire pit, doing my best to look serene.

"No Sasha today?" are the first words out my mouth. Damn. There goes serene.

Yan grins like I've told a hilarious joke. "She couldn't make it. But I'll tell her you said hi."

Awesome. I force a smile and step around a troubled Aleksi. He stares anywhere but into my eyes, and I pretend not to hear Yan as I wander round the edge of the group.

97

Guess it's my turn to be the dirty little secret. I can see why it pissed him off so much.

When I throw myself down into the empty chair next to Kamran, he shuffles his own closer. He leans over, his lawn chair letting out a tortured squeak, to murmur in my ear.

"Did Aleksi tell you he was coming?"

I shake my head, my mouth sour. Without a word, I pluck the mug of tea from Kamran's hand and take a scalding gulp.

Kamran grunts, frowning at our acrobat.

"How tedious."

"Tell me about it."

Yan chatters away—always the loud, outgoing brother next to Aleksi's quiet calm. Every now and then, Yan glances our way, his gaze lingering on Kamran's arm next to mine.

"How do you feel about petty stunts to make people jealous?" I ask, blowing on Kamran's tea before taking another sip.

A grin spreads over his sharp face.

"I was born to be petty, Hazelnut."

Kamran places his hand casually on my knee, like we sit this way every day. Yan doesn't notice at first, gesturing around at his audience. When he does, though, his eyes narrow, and Aleksi turns to see where he's looking.

Kamran smirks, his amber eyes vicious, and slides his palm higher.

"Whatever you're doing, cut it out."

Robbie glowers from Kamran's other side. I raise my eyebrows, taking another sip. I could really get into this tea.

"We're just minding our own business." I smile sweetly at Robbie. "What are you up to, boss man?"

"I'm warning one of my workers that she needs to find a partner."

Really? Talk about kicking a girl when she's down.

"I've put the word out," I say, voice icy. "I've got some auditions lined up."

Robbie grunts, his eyes flicking to where Kamran's hand still rests on my leg. When he looks up again, his blue eyes are hard.

"You're a paired performer, Hazel. Find a partner, or find another circus."

My mouth drops open, hurt rippling through my chest, but thankfully he's already gone. Kamran's rubbing my leg, whispering soothing words like I'm a horse, but I don't register any of it.

Robbie's put me on a ticking clock.

And when it runs out, I lose everything.

* * *

My least favorite sound in the world is Yan laughing in the breakfast line. Back before he screwed me over, before he cheated, dumped me, and dropped me mid-show, that sound used to warm me from the inside-out.

Now it just makes me want to stab his eyes out with a fork.

"Easy, tiger."

Kamran rests a cool palm on my shoulder. I glare at the back of Yan's head, tipped back as he crows with laughter. The chill autumn breeze tugs at my hair and whistles through the loose neckline of my sweatshirt.

I grumble under my breath, burrowing deeper into the fabric while the sweat from my workout cools on my skin.

It's bad enough that our three-year relationship ended the way it did. Why does he have to come back here? Why rub it in my face?

And to add insult to injury, Aleksi is always by his brother's side. He hushes him occasionally, sending me worried glances and digging an elbow into Yan's ribs, but we both know what this means.

Aleksi chose Yan. I was never really in the running.

Kamran wraps his arms around me from behind. I chew on the collar of my sweatshirt, leaning back against his warm chest.

"He's an asshole," I say through a mouthful of fabric.

Kamran nods, chin grazing the top of my head. "Which one?"

"Both of them."

Kamran waits until Aleksi and Yan glance over their shoulders then nibbles on my earlobe. Yan's eyes widen, his eyebrows shooting up his forehead, and I smirk.

Good. I hope the sight turns his stomach. Maybe he'll shut up for a minute.

Aleksi's watching us too, but he just looks tired.

I refuse to feel bad about that. Aleksi made his choices.

Still, I nudge Kamran away when the line shuffles forward. It's too damn early for all this posturing. I need coffee and a breakfast roll, stat.

If I think I'll get some space from the Genkov brothers, though, I'm dead wrong. The next three days are exactly the same: Yan and Aleksi are everywhere I look—by the food stalls, around the fire pits, in the tent. I don't ask Aleksi if he's training me while Yan's here, and he doesn't offer. They work through their own routines on the silks, soaring high overhead.

Fine. I duck my head and practice alone, a hard knot of anxiety in my chest.

"Do you want a hand?" Aleksi offers on the fourth day of

Yan's stay. "I could watch you, if you like."

I dust the excess chalk off my hands and grip the bar. My wrist twinges, same as always, but I ignore it.

"I really can't stress this enough, Aleksi." I address my knuckles, flexing my fingers to adjust my grip. "Fuck all the way off."

I don't start moving until he leaves, his footsteps muffled by the grass.

* * *

The silver lining with insomnia is that I have hours more time to practice. I haven't slept through the night since Robbie's threat—find a partner, or find another circus.

I've posted on forums, on social media, on industry websites. I've tapped old contacts and friends-of-friends. There just aren't that many trapeze artists knocking around in this part of the country.

Ginny seems to think that Robbie would let me stay on with the haunted house. That he's secretly a softie under that grumpy exterior.

I don't see it, personally. I think Ginny's been fooled by the accent.

Either way, the clock is ticking down, and with each passing day, I get less sleep. I lie in my bed, watching the shadows shift on the trailer walls, the trees creaking in the wind. The anxious knot in my chest seems to grow and grow, until it's blocking off the air to my throat and I have to get up or I'll explode.

It's the same every night. I tug on a sweatshirt, stuff my feet into my boots, and tiptoe out of the trailer. The walk through the dark, empty grounds makes my heart speed up and my palms sweat. I jerk my head around, half expecting another body to tackle me from behind.

By the time I slip inside the big top tent, I'm gasping for breath.

Training is a relief, after all that. It channels all the nervous energy burning through my body, and it focuses my mind. I run through every hold Aleksi and Yan taught me, and then I experiment with a few of my own.

Yan and I had a paired routine that we performed every night. I should run through that—as much as I can on my own—but instead, I find myself visualizing something else.

A solo routine.

Something beautiful and new.

I can almost hear the pounding of drums, the music the band could play. It whispers on the edge of my hearing as I grip the trapeze and swing.

I arc through the air, weightless and free. I'm still on the lowered practice stage, but if this was a show, if I was up there, under the spotlights—

I let go of the bar at the top of the arc and spin around, catching it on the way down. I'm fluid and flawless, dancing on the air, and the vice gripping my rib cage finally loosens an inch.

I was born to do this. The trapeze is where I belong.

There's a limit to what I can do without a partner, but it also brings opportunities. There's no one else competing for the best moves or the most attention—I can focus solely on the art. On the rise and fall of my body through the air, and the shapes my limbs make.

Yan choreographed our last routine. I've never done this

before. But once I start, it's like I'm walking down a path in my brain I've always known.

I know instinctively what should come next. I know how it will look, what will make the audience gasp. How to be daring, but unexpected.

I lower to the ground, arms shaking.

"Where did that come from?"

I suck in a breath. Robbie leans against the next platform, cloaked in shadows.

Heat floods through my body. That was so raw—my soul stripped bare. He might as well have marched into my trailer and watched me change—it would have been less intimate.

"Solo routine," I choke out. "For when I need to find a new circus."

Robbie says nothing; a statue in the shadows. My muscles tense up again, the knot reforming in my chest, and I hate him at this moment. He sneaked in here and stole my hard-won peace.

"Goodnight, boss," I spit, snatching up my sweatshirt and jumping off the platform. I stride across the grass towards the exit, a weird ringing in my ears.

Robbie hand clamps around my elbow and spins me around.

"Don't audition anywhere else. Not yet."

His words are urgent, but his face is blank. Only the muscle leaping in his temple gives him away.

I snatch my arm out of his grip.

"It doesn't work like that, Robbie. You can't threaten to kick me out then get pissed when I do something about it."

"I know." He rubs a hand over the scruff on his chin. "I know."

I wait for him to say something else, but he just stands there, watching me.

"Fun talk."

He blurts out his next words before I can turn away.

"I was… hasty. Before."

"That's one word for it."

Robbie sighs. "Don't rush to leave. I know how good you are, Hazel."

This is news to me, but I don't say so. Maybe because I'm only just starting to realize how good I could be myself.

"I don't want to leave." I lick my lips. "But I will if you mess me around."

I've never negotiated for myself like this. Stood up for my job, like a professional. My spine straightens and I tip my chin up. Robbie's blue eyes glint as they watch me, his broad chest rising and falling with each breath.

"Understood," he rasps, then he reaches for me. My lips part, the heat pounding in my core, but Robbie's eyes clear and he snatches his hand away.

It's too late, though. He can storm off, his hands shoved in his pockets. He can pretend all he likes.

I know he wants me too.

Chapter 10

I grab the last pieces of trash out of the haunted house train car, stuffing them in a garbage bag. People are animals when they come to the carnival. Litter is the least of our worries, but it still pisses me off to grab handfuls of greasy food wrappers.

"Ew."

Danika wrinkles her nose at the mustard-stained papers in my gloved hand. I wave it at her grinning and she dances away from the haunted house deck.

She's been checking on me every night since that creep cornered me alone in the dark. Between her and Ginny, I never lock up the ride alone anymore.

I love these women.

Tonight, though, Danika can head straight to the fire pits. She's not the first person to come poking around while I sweep up after closing.

"Danika!" Kamran pokes his head through the doorway, a fake cobweb caught on his dark curls. "Here to join in the fun?"

Danika snorts. "I don't think I could handle it."

Tipping her chin at me, she wanders away, chuckling to herself.

"Done back there?"

Kamran came to say hi after the show and I put him to work. If a hot guy is so keen to spend time with me that he'll willingly pick up a broom, I'm not going to tell him no. Especially since the second the leaves started dropping, they've been blowing in here on the breeze and gathering in drifts in the corners.

His smoky voice floats to me through the doorway.

"Come and see."

Kamran fucking loves the hall of mirrors. It has all his favorite things—an eerie atmosphere, chances to pickpocket, and his own reflection. I traipse through the doorway to find him, already patting my locket around my throat. My skeleton onesie is unzipped, the hood tipped back, and the gold heart rests against my sternum.

The hall of mirrors is empty. I wander deeper, my reflections walking with me on either side. The mirrors are tilted and warped so that no reflection is exactly the same, and they seem to echo my movements at different speeds.

"Come out, you creep."

Kamran steps out of the shadows behind me.

"That's no way to talk to your broom bitch."

His arms wind around me, dragging me against his bare chest. I watch him kiss my neck in the mirror, his amber eyes bright amid the kohl lining his eyes. My heartbeat thumps harder, and I feel it in my throat, my wrists, my clit.

A throat clears behind us. Reflected in the mirrors, Aleksi loiters in the doorway.

I sigh. "Can we help you with something?"

Kamran keeps nibbling at my neck, and I don't push him off. Why should I?

Aleksi's mouth sets in a firm line.

"I'd like to speak with you."

Kamran hums, the vibration tickling my skin.

"There are lots of things you'd like to do with her," he says, loud enough for Aleksi to hear. Aleksi huffs but steps forward, his boots heavy on the metal floor.

"Hazel. Please."

His reflection looks so damn miserable that I gust out a sigh and nudge Kamran off. When I turn and face the real him, Aleksi holds out both palms.

"I know Yan hurt you—"

"Not just Yan," I interrupt. Aleksi grimaces. His cheeks are still flushed from his show.

"Right. I hurt you too."

He says nothing else for a long stretch, and I raise my eyebrows. Surely that's not all.

"Is there a 'but' there? Anything else to say?"

"I miss you," he blurts out. "I wanted to see you."

I open my mouth and close it again.

I hate that my heart flips in my chest when Aleksi says those words. When he looks at me like that, his brown eyes shadowed with longing, his hands reaching for me from the doorway.

"You've been a prick," I say flatly. Aleksi nods, stepping closer. "You brushed me off for your brother."

"I didn't want to hurt him."

"No. So you hurt me instead."

Aleksi stands still, rubbing the bridge of his nose.

"Whatever I do, someone gets hurt."

I nod. "Yes."

That's about the size of it. Kamran shrugs, lounging against a mirror.

"Life is full of disappointments. How are you going to make it up to her, Genkov?"

I start to argue, not sure I want it made up to me, but Aleksi strides forward and cups my jaw with his hands. He's still burning hot from performing under the lights, his blood thrumming under his skin.

"Forgive me."

He traces his nose along my cheek but doesn't kiss me—not yet. Instead, he steers us back towards the mirrors, pushing me against Kamran's chest. Kamran grunts, taken by surprise for once, but his hands latch onto my hips.

"Forgive me," Aleksi says again, then presses his lips to mine.

It's nothing like the kisses we've shared before, battling for dominance. It's gentle, tentative— sweet, apart from the line of Kamran's cock digging into my spine. My lips part and I kiss him back, tangling my hands in his hair.

"This doesn't mean I'm not still pissed off," I murmur when he kisses along my jaw. Kamran rests his chin against my temple, content to let us use him as a wall.

"I know." Aleksi draws his head back and holds my gaze, face intense. "I'll make it up to you."

Kamran chuckles, and a smirk twists my mouth.

"How exactly will you—"

"Aleksi?"

All of Yan's reflections in the mirrors are pale and shocked. He blinks at the three of us, sandwiched together, my hands tangled in his brother's hair.

Aleksi inhales sharply and steps back, but the damage is done. Yan crashes back through the doorway, a sea of our flushed faces watching him go.

* * *

108

For as long as I've known them, Aleksi and Yan have only ever had each other. When the workers start reminiscing about home late at night, the brothers never chime in or mention their family. I tried to ask a few times, in the early days of dating Yan, but he gently shut me down each time.

"The past is not important," he said once when we were lying on the narrow bed in his trailer. He hooked an arm beneath my ribs and scooped me up so I was straddling him. The hard planes of his stomach beneath my thighs always made me hot and breathless. "The only way is forward."

I should have guessed that eventually I'd be relegated to the past too.

But the way he looked at me in that hall of mirrors, pressed between Kamran Lajani and his brother—it was like Yan had never seen me before in his life.

Yan's heavy steps thunder across the haunted house deck, and the three of us stand frozen, listening.

"Um." Aleksi's face is ghostly pale, his cheeks drained of blood, and I tug the sleeve of his black sweater. "Go after him."

Aleksi jerks his head to look at me, his eyes wide. He looks like he's waiting for us to pinch him so he can wake up.

Regret curls in my stomach. I knew why Aleksi didn't want to be with me. Yan is his world. I knew that, and I pushed him anyway.

Now he's staring at the door with that dazed expression, and all I can do is nudge him forward.

"Go find Yan. Talk to him. He's your brother, Aleksi, he loves you."

"He loved you too," Aleksi murmurs, and I swallow hard.

It's true. Yan loved me fiercely once, and look where we are now.

"Go," Kamran says, firmer than me, and Aleksi finally traipses out the door. I feel Kamran slump against the mirror behind me, the tension bleeding out of his chest. His thumbs stroke my hips, and I tip my head back against his shoulder.

"On a scale of one to ten, how much of this is our fault?"

Kamran hums, the vibration tickling my shoulder blades.

"Perhaps a five."

I start to argue, but Kamran interrupts me.

"Aleksi is a grown man, and he makes his own decisions. Neither the credit nor the blame is ours."

I gust out a sigh. "That sounds like the crap from the fortune teller's tent."

Kamran snickers. "Word for word."

The outside world is waiting for us. The reality of what we've done—the havoc we've caused. I'm not sorry, exactly—I don't owe Yan a damn thing, and he should want his brother to be happy. But the thought of dealing with the fall-out weighs on my tired limbs.

Just five more minutes.

"Come on, heart breaker."

Kamran nudges me off his chest and wraps his hand around mine. I let him lead me out of the haunted house like a little kid, leaning against the train car and watching him finish the lock-up with a slight smile.

"I can do that myself, you know."

Kamran shrugs, snapping the padlock into place.

"Let's hope so, Hazelnut. This has been your only job for months."

Raised voices echo through the night air as we weave between food stands to the trailers. Our breath fogs as we walk, the stars bright overhead, and I wish for a moment that

Yan would shut the hell up and look around.

It's harder to be an asshole when you focus on the beautiful things. The whisper of the breeze in the tree line. The scent of wood smoke on the air.

Or maybe Kamran's fortune teller crap is rubbing off on me.

It doesn't take a genius to guess who's doing all the yelling. Sure enough, as we near the fire pits, I catch sight of his shoulder-length chestnut hair.

Aleksi and Yan really could be twins. Except Aleksi has a few inches on him—in height, in hair length, and I now know in other areas too.

Yan yells, putting on a show for everyone clustered around the fires, and Aleksi just stands there and takes it. I wish for once he wouldn't be the better person—that he'd sock Yan in the jaw and shut the asshole up.

Robbie flings his trailer door open as we pass, glaring around for the source of the disturbance.

"Fucking hell," he mutters, pounding down the metal steps and striding towards the fire pits. Yan keeps ranting at the silent Aleksi, waving his arms in the air.

"Did you know? What they're up to in your precious carnival?" Yan rounds on Robbie as the three of us arrive. He jerks his chin at Kamran and me. "Did you know about their fucking threesome?"

Robbie scoffs and answers loud so everyone can hear.

"This is the circus, Yan, not Sunday service. I don't give a shit."

His hands ball into fists, though, before he shoves them deep in his pockets.

Yan sneers, his face twisted into a grimace. "Not even if they're fucking on a kid's ride?"

I splutter, cheeks flaming as dozens of heads swing around to stare at us. It's not even fucking true, but anything we say now will sound like a lie.

Robbie looks at us too, his eyes pausing on Kamran first, then me. I give him a tiny shake of my head, willing him to believe me.

I've been on thin ice here since the day Yan dropped me. Now I've finally found my feet again, working on routines, getting back in the air, and Yan is trying to ruin it for me again.

I don't fucking think so.

"It's none of your business." I speak up before Robbie has to deal with that bombshell. My voice comes out steady, even as my heart leaps into my throat. "If it bothers you, go moan to Sasha about it. No one here cares."

I seriously hope no one cares, anyway. Ginny calls out "Hear, hear," from the next fire pit over, and I shoot her a grateful smile.

Yan's not done with us yet, though. He always had a vicious streak. He flicks his hair back over his shoulder, eyes darting to Aleksi before they settle back on me.

"I suppose I should be flattered, Hazel. You need two men to replace me."

I grit my teeth, hand tightening around Kamran's, but Yan goes on, turning to his brother.

"You can do better than my sloppy seconds, Aleksi. Everyone here can." He shoots me a vicious grin and raises his voice, calling out to the grounds. "But if anyone needs their bed warmed, Hazel is open for business."

Hurt slams into my chest and steals my breath. Those faces all turn to look at me again—with pity, with disgust, with hunger—and I'm wrenched back to that night in the shadows, when that man barged me to the ground.

He called me a slut, and he put his hands on me.

Kamran squeezes my hand hard, and I suck in a painful breath.

I should be yelling, fighting back, reaming Yan out, but my lips are numb and my head spins. Muffled, on the edge of my hearing, I can hear Robbie barking out something, and the thud of a fist hitting flesh. I squint over at Yan like I'm in a dream, the flames dancing, and find him gone. Aleksi stands there instead, shaking out his hand.

"Let's go."

I turn, expecting to find Kamran, but it's Robbie at my side. I glance around, but Kamran is with Yan, a hand on his shoulder. My chest burns, and I drag in another breath.

"Hazel. Let's go."

Robbie grips my elbow and steers me away from the fire pits. The sea of faces swims in my vision and I stumble on the grass.

"Easy. You're okay."

Robbie doesn't lead me to his own trailer—I guess he doesn't want the rumors Yan just guaranteed. He leads me past my own trailer, too, and I frown at the scuffed door.

"Where are we going?" I mumble, voice so thick that I sound drunk. I don't know what the hell's wrong with me—only that when the memories of that night slammed into me, they dragged me somewhere dark in my brain.

"Not far."

We pause a short distance away at the steps of a silver trailer. The door is closed, the lights off inside, but Robbie nudges me up the steps and pushes the door open in front of me.

I stumble into a place I've never seen before: Kamran Lajani's trailer.

* * *

Sounds echo to me after a delay, muffled like I'm underwater, and I blink my eyes hard to focus. Fierce curiosity about Kamran's natural habitat has gnawed my insides for weeks. He never offered to bring me here, so I never asked, but now that I'm through the door I want to soak it all in.

The first thing I notice is how little furniture there is. There's no kitchen table, no sofa, no bed. Or at least, there are versions of those things, but not where you expect them.

Instead of a sofa, giant floor cushions surround a square coffee table. Where the bed should be, there's a hammock slung from the ceiling, and a mattress covered in pillows and blankets on the floor beneath. Kamran's elected for space over clutter—the only real trinkets on view are the silk scarves tossed over lampshades, and the bowl of oranges resting in the center of the coffee table.

His fire-eating equipment rests against the wall in the corner, and the smell of smoke and jasmine laces the room.

"Should we be in here?" I mumble as Robbie steers me to a floor cushion. He moves like he's familiar with the space, like he's been here many times before, and a thousand questions burn on my tongue.

What does he do here with Kamran? Does he want the fire-eater too? Jealousy spikes in my gut at the thought, but the image of being pressed between them soothes the acid away and replaces it with a throb in my core.

Robbie settles me down in silence, ignoring my question. He kneels in front of me, frowning into my eyes, his piercing blue gaze searching.

"What's going on, Hazel?"

His Scottish accent is so soft. I could wrap myself up in his voice and go to sleep.

"Nothing. I'm good." My teeth chatter. "Yan's just a prick."

Robbie grunts in agreement but shifts his weight, tucking away a strand of my hair. The pads of his fingertips linger on the shell of my ear.

"That's not what this is. You're not well."

I suck in a breath, steeling myself to tell him about the memories. About the nightmares. About how that night haunts me—what might have happened, if Robbie didn't find us in time.

I open my mouth, but no words come out. Instead, my face crumples. I fold in on myself, a red-faced, weeping mess, and I don't even realize Robbie's gathered me in his arms until I sniff and get a nose full of fabric. His shoulder is rounded and firm under my face, and I press myself closer, heedless of the wet patch I'm leaving behind.

"It's that night, isn't it?" Robbie mutters in my ear. "That prick by the food stalls?"

I nod, sobbing with relief that I don't have to say it. Robbie curses and holds me closer, not letting go even when the door creaks open and Kamran steps inside.

"There you are, Hazelnut."

If Kamran is surprised to find we've invaded his home, he doesn't show it. He wanders past us, his fingers dancing through my hair, then potters around to boil water for tea. He flicks on a couple of lamps as he goes, filling the space with a pink-tinged glow.

I sniff hard against Robbie's shoulder, clutching his shirt in my damp palms. The worst of the tension has bled from my chest, my heart rate slowing, but a shameless part of me wants to keep crying so Robbie will hold me longer.

As if he can sense my treachery, Robbie eases away.

"There you go." He murmurs soothing nonsense. "You're all right now."

I hiccup, wiping my snotty nose on my sleeve.

Goodbye, final scraps of my dignity.

"Yan will be gone by morning." Robbie's voice is almost as hard as his eyes. "He's not welcome here again."

Sorrow for Aleksi washes over me and I nod, too tired to be glad.

Yan is Aleksi's only family. How long will he stay here, where his brother can't visit?

"We weren't screwing on the ride." I don't know what else to say. Kamran snorts in his tiny kitchen, a teaspoon clinking against the china of his mugs.

Robbie sounds strained when he replies. "Duly noted."

Now that I'm coming back to myself, I notice more. Like how Robbie's eyes keep flicking towards Kamran's back. Like the flush darkening his pale cheeks, and the stiff way he's sitting.

Our boss is full of shit.

"Here." I crawl into his lap before he can protest, winding my arms around his neck. Robbie goes still as a statue beneath me, his muscled thighs hard beneath my ass. "I'm not done being coddled. You missed a bit."

Kamran tosses his head back and laughs, the sound bouncing around his kitchen. Robbie grumbles, but after a pause, his arms slide back around me.

"I can't have favorites," he grinds out. "Don't tell anyone about this."

"Our lips are sealed." Kamran emerges from the kitchen, three mugs clasped in his hands. Wisps of steam curl above each rim, and he places them on the coffee table with a thud.

When Kamran's eyes rake over my arms around Robbie's neck, his hands gripping my sides, he looks suddenly tired. He lowers himself onto a floor cushion far away from us, tucking his mug against his chin.

"Kamran," I say. His gaze flicks to me. "Thank you."

He nods, taking a sip.

Tension stretches between the three of us, expanding to fill the trailer until I can't stand it any longer. I hold out a hand to Kamran, the other fisting Robbie's shirt.

"Come here," I whisper, feeling Robbie's heart pound in his chest. Kamran looks at us, his mouth twisted to one side, but he relents with a sigh. He sets his mug down on the wooden table with a thud, then crawls over to our cushion.

I loop an arm around Kamran's neck and tug him until he's pressed against my other side. He moves gingerly, careful to only touch me and not Robbie.

We settle in awkwardly, limbs rigid and backs tense. I'm about to give up and nudge them both away again when Robbie grunts beneath me and snakes an arm towards Kamran. He grips the other man by the shoulder, pulling him closer, then slides a palm up his neck. I watch from inches away as they stare at each other, chests heaving, pupils blown wide.

A voice yells outside the trailer, and all three of us jump apart. It's nothing—a random worker who's had too much to drink—but the spell has been broken. We slide onto separate cushions, reaching for our teas, three shades of blush staining our cheeks.

At least Robbie doesn't leave this time. And at least Kamran doesn't shuffle back to his corner. We sit together, sipping in silence at first, then chatting about nothing. At one point,

Kamran rummages in his pocket and places Yan's watch on the table. I blink at it then howl with laughter, the back of my head thudding against the trailer wall.

Robbie rolls his eyes, but his lips twitch. He's shown his hand, our stern-faced boss. He stays with us, chatting and laughing until the early hours of the morning. And all the sickly fear that filled my veins at Yan's words slowly drains away until I'm warm and peaceful. Happy again.

Happy except for the hole gnawing at my chest for Aleksi.

He should be here. I feel his absence like a phantom limb.

And Yan's warning to him echoes through my head—*you can do better, Aleksi.*

Chapter 11

Aleksi doesn't mention his brother so I don't bring him up either. He slips back into training me every morning like he never stopped, the shadows under his eyes the only sign that anything ever changed.

"You don't have to do this," I tell him for the thousandth time. Aleksi shakes his head, stifling a yawn with his sleeve, and clears his throat.

"Try it again."

I go through the static poses, flowing easily between each one. My hands grip the bar tight, and my muscles burn, but I'm in control. My wrist still throbs now and then, a constant reminder of my fall, but I'm nearly back to full strength. In a few short weeks, I could perform.

I bite my lip against the smile stretching my mouth. It's been a long fucking road. And though I'm thrilled to finally make progress, to get my life back on track, I do miss the feel of Aleksi's strong hands bracing my waist.

"Feel free to step in." I wink at him, upside down. "You can correct my form any time."

Aleksi shifts from foot to foot, but doesn't move from his spot on the corner of the stage.

He hasn't touched me since Yan was here.

Robbie and Kamran join our practice after a while, like they've begun to do every morning. They enter together, murmuring to each other and breaking into laughter.

Kamran offers a coffee to Aleksi when they reach the platform, his elegant hand holding the steaming mug aloft. Aleksi nods at him easily, jumping down to stand at their side.

All three of them watch me together as I flow around the trapeze bar. I melt between poses, strong and sensual, feeling the rightness of every movement down to my bones.

I was born to do this. I want to show them what I can do.

Without a word of warning, I launch into my solo routine. I've been working on it every sleepless night, which is more nights than not. Each night that I practice, I hone a movement or perfect a series of poses. I build up to more ambitious movements, soaring higher, daring new twists and flips.

The three men stand in silence as I show them a piece of my soul. They don't speak a word, not until my feet touch back on the stage and I let go of the trapeze, breathing hard.

"What do you think?" I prompt after a moment, nerves churning in my gut.

Maybe it's not as good as I think. Maybe they're trying to find the words to let me down kindly.

"Gorgeous." Kamran is the first to speak. Aleksi nods at his shoulder, lips pressed tight. "People will come from miles to watch you."

I suck in a breath and turn to Robbie.

"Well?"

He's the one I really need to impress. Robbie strokes a hand over his chin.

"Show me without the harness," he says at last.

I nod, heart thundering.

I haven't practiced without the safety harness since I broke my wrist. For a split second, I can feel it—the air whistling by me as I fall, the sickening crunch of bone as I hit the ground. I breathe in hard through my nose, coming back to myself to find Aleksi frowning at me, his forehead creased.

"I've got it," I mutter, fiddling with the straps on the harness. My clumsy fingers take forever, but I finally shove the harness down my thighs and ankles and kick it down to the dirt.

Slow breaths.

In and out.

I've got this.

I cake my hands with chalk, conscious that my palms are already sweating. My wrist twinges as I brush my fingers together, as if to remind me of what happened last time I went up there without a harness.

Yeah, no shit. Not helpful.

I push those memories away, wiping my sticky forehead with my arm. Breathing in deep through my nose, I hold the air in my lungs for five counts before letting it out in a gust.

My fingers clench the trapeze bar, and I force myself to loosen my grip. I'll be useless if I'm stuck to the bar, clinging like a monkey.

I flex each finger, one by one, and shift my weight between my feet.

Three faces watch me from the ground. Kamran cocks his head to one side; Aleksi frowns and crosses his arms. Robbie's face is unreadable, his hands shoved in his pockets.

I take one final lungful of air and launch myself off the ground.

It's… fine. Exactly the same as my run through five minutes ago. I go through the moves, teeth clenched against the nerves

121

rising in my throat. I'm executing each move correctly, placing my limbs in the proper position, but every time the trapeze soars high in the air, my lungs seize in my chest.

I let go of the bar, flipping around and catching it on the way down. I grab it fine, but my palms are slick with sweat. I swing through to the other side of the arc, gripping the bar tighter. Something's not right—my fingers slide half an inch—

I bail on the lowest point of the swing, crashing to the ground. I land on my feet but stagger from the impact, the stage groaning in protest. Aleksi jerks forward, leaping onto the platform while Kamran's face falls.

Robbie sighs and looks at the ground.

My heart sinks.

"I'll work on it." I shrug Aleksi's hand off my shoulder, eyes fixed on Robbie. "I can do it. That was only my first try."

When Robbie looks up again, the cautious warmth we've been building is gone. We're back to boss and employee, his handsome face stern.

"I can't wait forever, Hazel. The circus needs a trapeze act." I give a jerky nod, wrapping my arms around myself, and his face softens. "Keep practicing. I'll give you a few more weeks."

He's being nicer than he needs to be, I know that, but his words still sting. I chew on the inside of my cheek, jumping down off the stage. Kamran tries to catch my eye while Aleksi drops behind me, but I ignore them both. I force a smile for Robbie, then I take off for the canvas door.

That was it. My chance. My big break.

And I blew it.

* * *

122

Danika finds me hours later after the night's meeting, curled up in a giant teacup. I'm in my skeleton onesie, a bottle of whiskey clutched in one fist as I rest my head on the rim.

"Oh dear."

Danika climbs onto the teacup ride deck, weaving between giant saucers. I'm surprised more workers don't come here to drink—it's damn comfortable.

"Pull up a teacup," I call, but she clambers into mine. Lowering herself onto the plastic bench opposite, Danika wrinkles her nose at the puddles of rain on the seat.

It's a kid's ride, obviously, with metal hoops in the center of each teacup. The ride spins you around in circles, and you can heave on the metal hoop to go faster.

Danika wraps her hands around the metal, and I scoff.

"It's too heavy," I start to say, but I'm forgetting that my roomie is surprisingly jacked. She heaves against the metal, her core twisting, then grunts as we start to spin. I lean forward, pushing on the hoop with my spare hand to help get us going.

The stars blur as we spin, sliding into lines, and the whiskey in my stomach lurches.

"Nope."

I sit back and wedge the bottle between my boots, squeezing my eyes shut.

"Stop it, woman."

Danika snorts but pulls us to a stop. We sit in silence, staring up at the stars as I try not to puke.

"Why the pity party?"

Her tone is light, but when I glance over there are worry lines creasing her eyes. Somewhere between my bratty start and all the awkwardness since, we've built something real.

"I auditioned for Robbie today." I chew my lip, resting my

123

head back with a thump. "I screwed it. Got freaked out and jumped off part way."

Danika doesn't say anything for a moment, and I brace myself for a pep talk. I know I need to stick at it and have faith. It still feels shitty.

Danika surprises me, though.

"Damn. That sucks."

That's all she says. No motivational slogans. No bumper-sticker platitudes.

I raise my head to frown at her.

"That's it? That's all you got?"

Danika shrugs. "You'll figure it out."

… Okay, then. I guess I will.

I grin, suddenly lighter. "What's your biggest career fuck-up?"

Danika is still a mystery to me. I know that she's a roadie, obviously, and I know her name is German. She has a faint accent when she speaks.

But people come to the circus from anywhere and everywhere, from all walks of life. We've got ex-cons and we've got rich kids running away from their families' expectations. There's a stall vendor who's also a published poet, and the man running the trucks was once a Hollywood star.

Danika taps her bottom lip. "I nearly burned down the astrophysics lab during my doctorate. That was bad."

I gape across the teacup. Slamming my mouth shut, I snatch the bottle from between my feet and take another swig. For a moment, I'm hit with the piercing knowledge that I'm small, and the universe is enormous, and even the people around me contain multitudes I'll never fully know. It's a dizzying sensation, and I wipe my mouth on my sleeve.

"What else don't I know about you?"

"I'm afraid of bees."

We rest our feet on the metal hoop and chat for hours, passing the bottle back and forth. I learn more about my roommate in one night than I learned in all the months prior.

One tidbit of information has me jolting upright in my seat.

"You were in a menage? You had two boyfriends?"

Danika prickles. "Yes. Aren't you shooting for three?"

"What happened?" I ask, ignoring her jab. I know that polyamory is a thing, and that couples aren't the only type of relationship. But I've never met anyone else who's tried it. I need the details.

"We grew apart, like any other relationship." Danika shrugs. "It happens."

That's so not enough. I need to know who, why, when, but first—

"How did you all get together?"

Danika smirks. "Looking for tips?"

"Yes," I tell her baldly.

She tips her head back and laughs, her bobbed brown curls splaying over the plastic rim of the teacup.

"It's the same as your trapeze problem," she says at last, passing the whiskey bottle. "You'll figure it out. Just be brave."

Be brave.

The whiskey burns through my veins and warms me from the inside out. I'm not drunk—just bright and bold, my rough edges sanded off.

I stand, take a final swig from the bottle, and pass it back.

"Right. Be brave. I can do that."

* * *

It's long past midnight, but crowds still throng around the fire pits. I wander between the lawn chairs and benches, breathing in wood smoke. I'm looking for a very particular person.

I find him sitting on an upturned barrel, one knee tucked under his chin.

Kamran Lajani.

"Come with me."

I slip my hand into his and pull him down off the barrel. He hops onto the grass without a fuss, letting me lead him away from the crowds. Whoops and wolf whistles fill the night air behind us, but my steps don't falter. I lead Kamran between all the fire pits, past trailers and food stands. I take him all the way to his own door, then look at him with raised eyebrows.

"Well?" The liquor makes me bold, and I push up onto my toes. I drag the tip of my nose along his jawline to whisper in his ear. "Are you going to invite me in?"

Kamran smirks, his amber eyes dancing as he leads the way up the steps. He never locks the door to his trailer—stealing from Kamran would be like throwing the first punch at Muhammad Ali—and it swings open easily under his palm.

I follow him inside, glancing around as he flicks on a lamp. The memory of being pressed between Robbie and Kamran—the way Robbie cupped Kamran's neck—makes heat pool between my legs. My clit starts to throb.

I look over and find Kamran staring at the same pillow, his gaze searing.

"He wants you too." Kamran jerks at my words, his jaw clenching as he turns to me. I lick my lips, my mouth suddenly dry. "I know it. He knows it. Probably half the roadies know it."

"I don't want to talk about Robbie right now." Kamran

prowls towards me, skating his palms up the outside of my arms. Goosebumps prickle on my skin underneath my clothes, blazing a trail everywhere he touches. "I only want you."

His kiss is fierce, claiming. I sway backwards with the force of it, clinging to his sweater. My skeleton mask scrapes over my back where it's dangling from my neck.

Kamran chuckles, tugging the piece of plastic over my head and tossing it to the floor. His eyes rake over my fleece onesie and boots, his lips curling on one side.

"Excellent choice of outfit, Hazelnut. One of your most seductive."

"Shut up."

I wish I could tease him for the same thing, but Kamran always looks sinful. Even now, in a midnight blue sweater and dark jeans, he looks tailored and delicious.

When Kamran looks rumpled, it's a designer kind of messy. When I do, I look like a hobo.

I back up a few steps, holding my palms out.

"If you prefer, I'll come back another time…"

Kamran growls and lunges forward, snatching me against his chest.

"Oh, no you don't. You're not leaving my sight. Not until I've peeled this hideous costume off and made you scream."

Well, when he puts it like that.

I nip at his chin. "You're all words, Lajani. Show me."

Kamran doesn't need to be told twice. He scoops me into his arms, hands planted on my ass. I wrap my legs around his waist and wind my arms around his neck, and he walks us towards the mattress in the corner.

He stops, ready for me to hop down, but I'm not done up here just yet. I cling a little tighter, sucking on his bottom lip and grinning when he groans. The sound reverberates through his chest, all the way to my core, and I feel myself getting damp in my panties. Swollen and slick with want.

"Get down, you evil sprite."

I drop to the floor, still mouthing at his throat. Kamran lets out a shaky breath and drags the zip down on my onesie.

Underneath, I'm in my leggings and a t-shirt, my tattoos peeking out from my sleeves. Kamran peels the onesie off my shoulders, impatient to reach the next layer.

"You're like that birthday game with all the wrapping paper."

I kick my boots off and step out of the puddled fleece.

"If you dig far enough, you'll reach a pack of Twizzlers."

Kamran snorts. "I don't want to know where you're keeping those."

He kneels to slide my leggings down my thighs, and I run my fingers through his glossy black hair. It's soft against the calluses on my hands, the strands curling around my knuckles. I scratch lightly at his scalp, and a shudder runs through his body. He leans forward to graze his teeth over my bare thigh, his hands peeling off my socks.

As soon as he's done, I yank him to his feet and pull the sweater over his head. He's so much taller, I can't fully reach, and Kamran takes over, dropping it at our feet. His t-shirt is next, even as I bat his hands away from mine. I don't care whose turn it is—I want to see him. Every glorious inch of his broad chest. Dark hair dusts the skin, and his nipples are deep brown. I lick a stripe over one, raking my nails down his stomach.

"Fuck." He pulls my hands away and yanks my t-shirt over my head. I'm left in just my bra and panties, while he still wears his jeans. "Give me a fighting chance."

"Lose the pants, then."

He does as I say, his fingers quick and sure on the buttons. I stare shamelessly at every new inch of bare skin, and at the tenting in his black boxers. Stepping close, I rub the outline of his cock, shivering when it jumps in my palm.

"God," I mumble as he hisses in my ear.

"Not quite," he croaks. "Close, though."

I roll my eyes and push at his chest, sending him crashing down on the mattress. He watches me with searing eyes as I tug my panties over my hips and drop them to the floor. He tugs his boxers off as I flick the clasp of my bra, and then we're both naked.

So much bare skin. So many muscles and tendons; I could catalogue his body all day. The way his eyes burn hot over my body, Kamran feels the same way. I straighten my spine, the power making my head spin.

Kamran's cock juts out towards his abdomen, a bead of pre-cum on the tip.

"Stroke yourself."

His hand wraps around the base, stroking from root to tip. Kamran flicks his thumb over the head, smearing the moisture there.

"That's it," I murmur, biting my lip. I skate a palm down my own bare stomach and slide a finger along my seam. I'm soaked.

I need him inside me right now.

"Condom?"

Kamran nods, rolling onto his side to fish a packet from the side of the bed. Once he's back and ready, his eyes fixed on mine, I straddle his hips and notch his cock at my entrance.

"Sure about this?"

Kamran rolls his eyes, then grips my hips and sinks me down on his length. I moan at the sudden fullness, at the slide of his cock in my body. He's a lot to take, and I have to work myself up and down a few times before he's completely inside.

"Fuck," Kamran groans once we're sealed tight together. "You're so fucking gorgeous."

I smooth a hand over his chest, along his jaw, and fist it in his hair.

"So are you," I breathe, and start to move.

With every rock of my hips against his, the pressure builds in my core. Kamran thrusts up, meeting me with every stroke, and I whimper at the sensation.

It's been months since I was with Yan, and even with him, it was never like this. Bliss flows through my body in waves, and I slam down on Kamran harder. I want him closer, deeper—I want to seal us together so we never come apart.

Kamran licks a stripe up my throat.

"That's it. Take what you want, Hazel."

The door slams open and we freeze on the mattress, staring at Robbie in the doorway. We're naked, our skin glistening with sweat, Kamran's cock lodged deep inside me.

"Get the fuck inside," Kamran grinds out, and Robbie jolts back to life. He enters fully, slamming the door shut behind him.

Robbie's shoulders heave, and for a moment none of us say anything. Kamran is still hard, still feels deliciously good, so I can't help it. I rock my hips.

Kamran groans, tossing his head back against the mattress, and I start to ride him again. I look over at Robbie, standing wide-eyed and rigid, and hold out a hand.

"Come here." I pour every ounce of command I can muster

130

into those two words. Robbie is not the sort of man to take orders, but he drifts towards us like he's in a trance.

"Here." I point to the mattress by Kamran's shoulder. "Kneel down."

He drops to his knees, staring at my breasts, at Kamran's stomach, at the cock sliding into my pussy. I reach over, still rocking my hips, and tug at Robbie's belt buckle.

"Off. Get this off."

Kamran turns his head on the mattress and watches with me as Robbie undoes his belt. He lets it hang loose, his fingers moving to flick his button open.

I glance down at Kamran at the same time he looks up at me. He huffs a laugh, his mouth quirking up at one side, and I lean down to kiss him hard. He thrusts his tongue into my mouth, and we rock together in our own world until the slide of a zipper brings us back to Earth.

Robbie's cock is paler than Kamran's. It's thicker, but not as long. I reach out a hand, waiting until Robbie nods before I slide my fist over the head. His skin is like velvet, scorching hot, and I groan, thrusting faster against Kamran.

I lower my head to lick at the tip of Robbie's cock. He curses softly above my head, and as I take him fully into my mouth, Kamran's hands grip my legs hard enough to bruise. My head bobs up and down as I suck Robbie's cock, and out of the corner of my eye I watch Kamran stare up at our boss.

God. They're both so gorgeous.

Robbie must agree, because his hand rakes through Kamran's curls, then drifts down to cup the side of his cheek. His thumb nudges at Kamran's plump mouth, and the fire eater sucks the digit fully inside.

Robbie groans, and Kamran tenses beneath me, swelling

131

inside my pussy. I grind harder against him, spots floating in my vision as I come so hard my whole body shudders. Kamran comes with me, and Robbie follows, pulsing inside my mouth.

I swallow it all down, gasping for breath when I finally sit up.

We blink at each other, chests heaving, the scent of sex heavy in the air.

"Did you need something?" Kamran asks Robbie eventually, and I crease forward, laughing into his chest.

Three separate hands smooth over my back, and I smile into his warm skin.

Hell yeah, Danika.

I can be brave.

Chapter 12

L iving in the circus is like living in a bubble. You forget, among the leaping flames and spinning rides, what it's like out in the real world.

Fucking dreary, apparently.

I slam Ginny's car door and squint around the parking lot. It's a cratered cement wilderness, dotted with piles of abandoned tires and a burned out school bus. Weeds grow in thick clumps, sprouting through the crumbling stone, and icy rain sleets down from dark clouds.

The end of the fucking earth.

The parking lot nestles between four industrial warehouses, giant walls of corrugated iron looming on all sides. I check the torn scrap of paper in my pocket—this is it. Auditions.

My last chance to stay on the trapeze if Robbie loses patience with me.

I leave the car between a battered Honda and a slumping motorbike. The address on the scrap of paper takes me to the smallest warehouse, tucked between a giant garage and a boxing gym. The shutters are rolled up so anyone can walk in, and I duck inside out of the rain with a shiver.

It's dim inside, and smells of mildew. As my eyes adjust, I notice the aerial equipment hanging from the warehouse ceiling: silks from one rafter, giant hoops from another. A trapeze from a third. A wobbly school desk is tucked against one wall, with a man in his thirties and an older woman sitting behind it.

The man looks like he's got the wrong desk. With his rolled shirt sleeves, polished glasses and sensible haircut, he seems more like an accountant than a circus freak. The woman, at least, has dyed turquoise hair and tattoos creeping up her neck.

"Frederica Johnson!" she rasps out in a smoker's growl. A nervous young woman in a leotard and tights hurries to the silks.

As Frederica shows what she can do, twisting and dancing up the silks without any music to help her, I wander to the desk. There's a sign-up sheet and a pencil, the nib snapped off.

"Um," I whisper to the accountant man. "Do you have a pen?"

He huffs like I'm the worst inconvenience of his life, but his fishes one out of his shirt pocket and hands it to me. I scrawl my name and act at the bottom of the list, passing the pen back and joining the crowd lining the other walls.

Here they are—here are my people. Freaks and acrobats; contortionists and con men. They slump against the rusting walls and sit cross-legged on the floor, dressed in a rainbow of bright colors like a flock of birds of paradise. I drop my satchel on the bare cement and kneel down beside it, the stone's chill seeping into my shins.

A man bends down next to me, whispering from behind a salt-and-pepper beard. With his slender shoulders and scarred face, he reminds me of a pirate.

"Contortionist?"

"Trapeze."

He nods and straightens up, chewing on a pat of tobacco as

he watches Frederica's audition.

Guess they're not a chatty bunch. I don't blame them; nerves curdle in my stomach and when I let myself think about going on that trapeze without a harness, my throat squeezes tight.

I'm more than happy to sit here and stew.

The auditions trundle along slowly. Each act has ten minutes to perform, then there's changeover time. For every performer who exits the warehouse, another couple walk in, until we're clumped thickly against the back wall. We pressed so tight together that we have our own micro-climate, warming the air with our bodies and breaths.

I stand, dodging elbows, and twist my spine until it cracks. Freezing down on that floor is a fool's move. I need to be ready, warm, limber. A few others have the same idea, breaking away to a corner to stretch and warm up. I grab my bag and follow, leaving the muggy warmth of the crowd for the freezing corner of the warehouse.

"Hazel?"

I glance up from my lunge, almost toppling to the cement when I see who it is.

Sasha Daniels.

The last time I saw Sasha, she was white-faced and shaking, staring down at my ruined wrist with Yan's arm wrapped around her shoulders.

Yeah, I bet she was super concerned. She really gave a shit about me when she ran off with my boyfriend and left me injured and alone.

"Perfect." I straighten up, brushing dust off my leggings. "Of course you're here. Is Yan here too?" I scan the crowds, searching for his long, chestnut hair.

"I don't know."

135

Sasha's voice is quiet. She bites her lip, hovering at my side. "Can you move the fuck along?"

Eyebrows rise around me when I snap, but screw it—I'm not here to make friends. I'm here to audition, to look for a partner, and to prove to myself I can still work the trapeze.

Sasha features in none of that. She nods, opening her mouth like she wants to say something, then moving along instead.

Good. I glare at the back of her blonde French braids as she drops her bag beside the wall. She braces a hand against the rusty metal and pulls up one ankle, stretching her thigh.

If she's here, where is Yan? Are they not partnered anymore? Did he dump her too?

No. I won't go down that rabbit hole.

I'm here for me.

By the time the smoker lady calls my name, I've already been through the five stages of grief.

"Hazel Harris!"

The woman's chainsaw growl cuts through the warehouse and sets my heart pounding. I dust my hands with chalk and cross to the trapeze under dozens of watchful eyes.

I grip the bar, flexing my fingers one by one, ignoring the twinge of my wrist.

A cough sounds at the back of the warehouse. I take a deep breath…

And jump.

* * *

"That was incredible."

Sasha's voice floats to me across the parking lot. I pause with my satchel slung on the roof of Ginny's car, one arm out of my sweatshirt. I scowl, watching her dodge puddles of rainwater as she nears.

"Thanks," I say eventually. There are a million other things I could say, the words ready on the tip of my tongue. But I don't want to burst the bubble I'm floating on right now.

I nailed it. That performance was everything my first audition should have been. Confident, graceful, daring, sure. I knew less than a minute in that I was smoking the competition, and when I crossed back to collect my bag afterwards, I basked under envious glares.

I shouldn't ask, but my curiosity gets the better of me.

"Did you go already?"

Sasha nods, chewing her thumbnail.

"I blew it. Didn't fall or anything, but I fumbled half the moves."

A mean voice whispers in my head that it serves her right. But I'm still flying high on my performance, and I offer a shrug.

"Can't win them all. I screwed my audition for Robbie last week."

Sasha's mouth quirks. "I can't believe he made you audition at all. He has a soft spot for you a mile wide."

How the hell she knows that when Robbie barely looked at me before she left is beyond me. When Sasha lived with us, I was with Yan every minute of the day, and Robbie didn't know I existed beyond the nights' shows.

Then she ran off with my boyfriend. Right. Forgot about that for a second.

"So, did Yan drop you too?" I can't stop the spite bleeding into my voice. But hey, she came over to me. I've been restrained so far.

"Yes, actually." Sasha twitches up the leg of her yoga

pants—an angry red scar twists around her calf.

"Jesus."

She hums, letting the fabric drop.

"Yan's a fucking butterfingers."

She snorts. "Yan's a lot of things."

For a second, I imagine Sasha's life over the last few months. Leaving her home of several years for a guy, then winding up in this tumbledown warehouse, alone and with a scar on her leg.

"Do you want to get a drink?" I blurt, regretting the words as soon as they're out. I open my mouth to take the offer back, but Sasha's nodding hard.

"Yes. Definitely. A thousand percent."

Fuck it. It's only a drink.

* * *

I pull back into the carnival grounds with Sasha's car in tow. It's dark, the sky dim with evening gloom, and the preparations for the night's crowds are just beginning. I circle the edge of the site, wincing every time Ginny's car bounces over a grassy knoll, and glancing at Sasha in my rear view mirror.

There's something wrong with me. I'm a sucker on a fundamental level. But after grabbing hot chocolate with Sasha and hearing the piss-poor time she's had of it, I blurted out that she should come back. You know: beg Robbie to let her work a stall until she's back on her feet.

Sasha beamed at me over her mountain of whipped cream like I was the second coming. And, okay, I guess I was still feeling magnanimous after nailing that audition.

Still, if she looks the wrong way at one of my guys... I will cut a bitch.

"I'd offer you the spare bed in my trailer," I lie once we're parked up, "but it's already taken."

Thank the lord for Danika.

"That's okay." Sasha stares around the sea of trailers and stands, workers darting across the grass. "I'll figure something out."

Neither of us mention the pillow and comforter bundled in her backseat. Whatever bed Sasha finds, it'll be an improvement.

I ditch Sasha at the first opportunity and set off looking for Aleksi. He's still being weird, hasn't touched me since Yan was here, but he's the first person I want to tell about my audition.

He's the one who got me back on the trapeze. The one who told me I should go solo.

It's early—there are still a few hours until the crowds arrive. Aleksi spends his off-time doing two things: training, and helping out at the food stalls.

He told me once that it's the thing he misses most from home. Cooking with his grandmother. That confession is the most he's ever told me about his life before the circus.

When I poke my head through the canvas flap, the big top tent is empty. It's eerie, when no one's there—like the sounds of the crowd are still trapped inside, bouncing around on the edge of hearing. I shiver and duck back into the spots of rain.

Icy sleet spatters my cheeks as I wander round the food stalls. He's not slicing onions with Ginny or mixing wisps of cotton candy. I frown, wiping my face on my sleeve, and stare around the sea of food stalls.

"He's with Kamran."

Robbie stands just behind me, beads of rain dusting his

stubble. I grin and reach up a hand to brush them away, but he steps back, shaking his head minutely.

The grin melts off my face as fast as it came. Right. No favorites for the boss.

"How did it go?"

His words are light, but his face is sour. Robbie's been sucking on a lemon since I told him I needed a day for auditions.

Whatever. It's his hang up, not mine. He's the one who keeps threatening to replace me.

"Fantastic." I sound smug, but I don't care. "I should get a few offers."

Robbie nods, eyes boring into the dirt. "Will you take one?"

"Depends whether I have a job here."

Robbie breathes in hard through his nose, but he doesn't look up from the ground. He doesn't say the words that would untangle this whole mess; won't tell me my job is safe.

He's the boss, first and foremost. A businessman, always. As far as he's seen, I'm a patchy performer. Fifty percent is not a success rate to brag about.

"Anyway." My smugness is gone, and I'm suddenly exhausted. "Sasha is here. She wants to work on a stall. She's been living in her car."

Robbie grunts, his eyes flicking up to me.

"And you're okay with that?"

I shrug. "I won't wish someone homeless."

The radio crackles on Robbie's belt, and then he's talking into it and striding away. I watch him go, my heart sore in my chest.

He'll never put me before the circus.

I find Aleksi and Kamran playing cards in the warmth of

Kamran's trailer. I toe off my boots, shucking my coat onto the floor, then crawl onto the cushions between them.

Kamran's thumb rubs circles on my ankle. After a long pause, Aleksi strokes a long strand of my hair.

"Have you seen Robbie?" Kamran asks, his voice casual, but I see the tense set of his shoulders.

I shake my head, burrowing deeper into the cushion.

"He's not coming," I tell him, voice muffled.

I watch them play, not bothering to join in. Instead, I let the hum of their conversation wash over me, until I doze off squeezed between their warmth. Gentle fingers stroking over my skin, tracing intricate patterns.

It's enough.

It has to be.

Chapter 13

I got cocky.

I rode high on the success of that one audition, and I let my guard down. I forgot the first rule of Cirque de la Lune: only a fool would trust in the circus.

Well, I'm a fool. I trusted I belonged here, that this was my home, and that I owned that spot on the trapeze. I trusted Robbie to care for me as a boss if not a boyfriend, and to protect my best interests.

Like I said. I've been a fool.

It's not long after the show when I duck inside the big top tent. Robbie just held court at the fire pits, delivering the nightly meeting, and we settled in afterwards to card games and dice and sleight of hand. One of the fortune tellers called me over, offered to read my palm, and I waved her off laughing, saying I preferred the surprise.

I only headed to the tent on a whim, to see if I left my favorite sweatshirt there.

My words to the fortune teller ring in my head as I take in the sight before me. The tent is shadowed, empty except for the two figures over on my platform. The heat from the crowd still lingers in the air, along with the muddy scent of grass. Aleksi killed it at the show tonight—I watched him from beside the speakers, my heart in my mouth even though I've seen his routine a thousand times. The wild applause of the crowd, the scent of all those bodies—the echoes hit me as I walk across the dirt.

Robbie stands on the edge of the platform, his arms crossed. And Sasha grips the trapeze bar, launching into the air.

I wait for him to tell her to get down. But of course, they planned to be here.

Sasha doesn't fumble this audition. Doesn't miss a single move. Every pose is deliberate and graceful, her slender body twisting overhead. Robbie watches her intently, the same way he watches me—his head tilted up and his eyes fixed on her every gesture. She soars through the air, and his gaze tracks her, the tent silent except for their breathing.

It's so fucking intimate, I can't stand it.

I watch him watching her, and my stomach lurches. I wrap my arms around my waist and force myself to keep quiet.

Sasha's routine has Yan written all over it. It's showy, daring, full of his signature explosive moves. He must have taught her some solo work before he dropped her, too.

It's another insult to add to the pile. Yan never bothered to teach me solo techniques. He only ever saw a partner in me—and a lesser one, at that.

My wrist throbs inside my sleeve, and I hug myself tighter.

Maybe this isn't what I think it is. Maybe I've got it all wrong. I step slowly into the shadows of the next platform where I can watch without risk of being seen.

When Sasha's feet touch back down on the floor, Robbie gives a brisk nod.

"Good." His voice echoes through the tent. My heart batters against my rib cage. "You're an excellent performer. Much

143

better without Yan."

He saw them practice together? When they were both still here?

Why didn't he tell me?

A horrible thought slides under my skin: that Robbie knew what was happening and said nothing. Knew that Yan was training with a new partner behind my back. Maybe even encouraged it.

"Good enough to headline?" Sasha asks between gasps, propping her hands on her hips. "Or I could partner Hazel. I don't want to edge her out."

Very fucking considerate of her. I clench my teeth so hard they creak.

Robbie grunts, like he's actually considering this. So much for giving me a few weeks to get back on the bar.

"I'll think about it."

Fuck. He's going along with this.

Blood roars in my ears, and I stumble backwards, my heel kicking an empty can. It skitters along the dirt; the sound echoing in the silent tent.

Two heads jerk around in my direction, but I'm sprinting for the door.

"Hazel!"

I've only heard Robbie yell like that once before. Urgent and desperate, like he's losing control and can't stand it.

He yelled like that the night I fell.

And he yells after me now.

I pump my legs faster, my boots catching in clumps of grass. When I burst out of the doorway, I wheel away from the lights of the trailers. He'll find me in minutes there, and I do not want to be found.

Not like this. Not with hurt radiating through my chest, and tears wetting my cheeks.

I pound over the empty field towards the tree line. Behind me, I hear Robbie burst out of the tent, and I slow my steps, keeping quiet.

I tug my black hood up over my hair, blending into the shadows. Knolls and hidden rabbit holes catch at my boots, but I stumble to the trees. Their branches reach high overhead, creaking in the wind.

The bark is rough against my palm as I lean against one to catch my breath. Turning, I watch the lights of the trailers. The columns of smoke twisting above the fire pits. One of the rides is still switched on, its colored lights flashing.

A hole yawns open in my chest, and I muffle a sob.

I turn my back on the circus and stumble through the trees.

* * *

Dawn paints the sky pink when I step into the field. I cross the grass, my teeth chattering. My head throbs from a night without sleep, and my skin is numb under my costume.

I needed this. Needed time to think. For hours, I wandered through the trees and gazed up at the stars. Ran what I'd seen over and over in my head. Considered what it means for me.

Now I'm chilled to the bone as I approach the trailers, the embers glowing in the fire pits. I cried for hours last night, endless heaving sobs, until I came out the other side, scoured clean.

My mind and body are tired, but I feel fresh. My path is clear.

This is not my home. It never was. It's a job, and it's a

great one, but no one here owes me anything. If I want to make a name for myself, if I want to perform solo routines for screaming crowds, I'm the only one who can make that happen.

Not Robbie. Not Yan. Not Aleksi, even though he might try.

Me. It all comes down to me, and what Danika told me that night in the teacup.

Time to be brave.

It's too early for anyone to be up. We're nocturnal creatures in the circus; even when I dragged myself out of bed to work out before dawn, I was the only person awake for miles. We're happiest in the darkness, in the small hours of the morning when everything gets fuzzy and wild.

I sniff, wiping my sleeve across my top lip. My nose has been running for hours; I'm courting sickness, staying out all night like this.

That's it, though. Enough drama. Enough bad decisions.

Like Robbie, I'm a professional. First and always.

I wince as my trailer door groans on its hinges. Toeing my boots off by the door, I pad to my bed and crawl under the covers fully clothed. My shivers are so violent, I nearly punch myself in the chin when I draw the blankets up to my head.

Warmth. Sleep. Food. In that order.

After that, I have a plan.

* * *

I wake to a pounding headache and a lukewarm mug of coffee by my bed. Danika left me a cold breakfast roll, wrapped in paper napkins. Her loopy handwriting catches my eye on the paper: *Robbie's looking for you. D.*

146

I shift under the covers, testing my limbs. They're aching and stiff from my night in the woods, but at least I've warmed up. Though the tip of my nose is freezing in the open air, under the covers, I'm an inferno. I shuffle up to lean against the headboard and notice Danika's quilt tossed on top of my own.

Moisture brims in my eyes and I blink hard.

I'll miss my roomie.

I've barely taken three bites of my breakfast roll before heavy boots thud up the trailer steps. I swallow hard, throat suddenly dry, and watch the doorway as Robbie barges inside.

"For fuck's sake."

He leaves the door hanging open and crosses to the bed. His all-knowing eyes track over my nest of quilts, my wild hair, my pale, tear-stained face. One hand fists in the quilt by my knee, squeezing until his knuckles go white.

"What were you thinking?"

My hackles rise. I was all set to be serene about this, to rise up and be the bigger person. But the second his low voice cuts through the silence, furious and demanding, all my hard-won calm goes flying out the doorway.

"I fancied a walk," I grit out, clenching my roll so hard that a sausage drops out the side.

"You could have been hurt. You could have been hypothermic. You could have gotten lost. Hell, you could have run into another psycho—"

"But I didn't. I stayed close to the camp, and got some fucking peace from you all."

Robbie closes his eyes, breathing in hard through his nose like I'm testing his very last nerve. Well, buddy, the feeling's mutual.

147

"Have you finished your little tantrum now?" he mutters.

"Yes," I bite out.

"Are you going to be a fucking adult about this?"

"Absolutely."

Robbie peeks out from one eye, rubbing a hand over his jaw. He looks at me again with fresh eyes, and this time he sees my straight shoulders. The glint in my tired eyes.

"Consider this my notice." Robbie's hand drops to his side. He blinks at me, dumbstruck, as I go on. "I'll clear out by breakfast tomorrow. Sasha can have my bed."

"That's not—she's—I'm not letting her replace you," he growls.

I snag my lukewarm coffee and take a sip, wrinkling my nose at the taste.

"It doesn't matter what you do with her. I'm gone either way."

Robbie opens and closes his mouth a few times. He rocks on his heels and glances at the door. Through the open doorway, curious faces peer in as they walk by.

The boss and the trapeze girl, alone in her trailer. Exactly what Robbie was so desperate to avoid.

He sighs and stomps over to the door, closing it with a snap.

"Don't do this." His eyes pleading with me across the trailer. "Don't throw everything you've worked for away."

I lift my chin, pushing my shoulders back.

"I'm not. I've had offers, Robbie. Several, in fact."

"Partner work?" he asks, face strained.

"Solo."

And there it is. He doesn't see me for the performer I could be—he only sees Yan's ex-girlfriend, dropped and spurned. Even if he hadn't auditioned Sasha, I needed to go anyway.

I need to prove I can do this. And when I do, no one will say it's because I'm sleeping with the boss.

Robbie nods, face miserable, and comes to kneel at my bedside. He gusts out a breath, tipping forward to rest his forehead against mine.

"Will you come back, Hazel?"

His breath fans across my cheek. I flex my fingers on my mug, my sore heart screaming for me to change my mind.

I shrug, my shoulder brushing his chin.

"No. I don't think so."

* * *

It takes me a depressingly short amount of time to pack up my trailer. Despite my offer, Robbie doesn't give anyone my bed. He comes in when I'm done to inspect the space, his nostrils flaring.

"I'll keep it open," he says at last, voice pitched low so only I can hear. Outside through the open doorway, a couple of the vendors cackle over a joke. "For whenever you come back."

I shrug and offer him a smile, but we both know what I'm thinking.

I'm leaving for good.

With the rest of the day stretching out in front of me, I gnaw on my bottom lip. I could sit around the fire pits with the roadies, or drag Kamran into his trailer to debauch him one last time.

I dismiss the thought as soon as it crosses my mind. My heart aches in my chest, and I know that if I fall into Kamran's arms, I'll never leave. My willpower is not that strong.

So I stay away.

I chop onions with Ginny. I play cards with Danika and chat in an empty teacup. I wander around the whole carnival site, every inch of it, taking in the sights and smells like it's the first time all over again. The brightness and the savagery. The feral joy.

The haunted house is a surprisingly rough goodbye. I work it one more time, even though Robbie tells me not to bother. I slip that skeleton onesie over my shoulders and swallow down a lump in my throat.

Jesus Christ. Here I am, getting sniffly over a lump of stinking fleece.

I throw myself into the work, losing myself in the rhythm of the ride. Loading kids and parents into the car, jumping out at them, ushering them off. It's slick, like clockwork—I've got this down to a fine art by now. I switch my brain off and pass the hours.

Sasha finds me after the show, when I'm sweeping out the litter to lock up.

"Robbie told me you're leaving."

She watches me from the grass beyond the deck, her slender body swallowed up by a massive hoodie. I nod tightly, biting back what I want to say.

He'll ask her to work the trapeze. I know that; I know it's a good business decision. It's nothing personal about me.

I still don't want to fucking hear it. I wish I never brought her back here.

"I wanted to thank you."

I shoot her a scathing look. "For clearing out of your way?"

"For giving me a second chance." Sasha shrugs, crossing her arms over her chest and gripping her elbows. "I was in a bad place and you helped me. I owe you."

I want to punch her; I want to toss my head back and laugh. But this isn't her fault—not really. She's just trying to survive, to make her own way like the rest of us.

No one ever said the circus was gentle.

"Make the most of it." I sweep a pile of dirt onto the grass. "Don't make Robbie regret it."

"I won't."

Sasha stands there a few minutes longer, but I'm done talking to her. I'm not a damn saint.

After the padlock's secured and streams of workers flow past, traipsing towards the fire pit, I slink away. I don't need to know how it went tonight. I won't ever need to know again.

Ever since my first season with the circus, I've had this crazy idea in the back of my mind. I swipe a bottle of beer from the bar stall and set off away from the crowds. I weave past the spinning teacups and the pirate ship; past flashing rides with tinny music.

On the edge of the grounds, I reach the Ferris wheel. I slide my beer bottle inside my onesie, tucking it in the waistband at the back of my leggings, and mutter a botched prayer.

Then I flex my chilly fingers and begin to climb.

I know it's dumb to risk falling when I'm just starting my career over. When there's no one nearby to hear me call for help.

But I didn't run away to the circus so I could make sensible choices. I came to feel alive.

I climb high enough that the wind tears through me. Until my fingers go numb and my muscles burn. Then, when I reach the highest carriage on the wheel, I topple inside. It jerks under my weight, swaying madly, and I fish my beer out of my leggings with a wince. The top screws off with a hiss, and I take a long pull of lukewarm goodness.

Yeah. This was an excellent bad idea.

I don't hear anyone else climbing until boots echo on the spokes halfway. I lean out of the open carriage, squinting down the Ferris wheel, and see the top of Aleksi's head. He surges upwards, muscles bulging in his powerful arms, his grip steady and sure.

I shuffle back to make space for him, and he crawls over the lip. He's not even out of breath, his hair tousled by the wind.

"Want some?"

I tip my beer towards him, and Aleksi accepts with a chuckle. He crawls on his knees to my side, pulling up to sit on the plastic bench.

We gaze out at the flames of the fire pits. At the stars shining overhead, and the dark patches of trees, and the lights of the city in the distance. Aleksi's shoulder is warm against mine, and I seal against him everywhere I can reach.

We haven't been this close since Yan visited. I've missed him so much.

"How'd you find me?" I ask as he tips the bottle back. His throat bobs as he swallows.

"I was walking around looking for you, and I saw the carriage swinging. Seemed like something Hazel Harris would do."

I grin and take the offered bottle. "And I thought I was so sneaky."

I take another long pull, then rest my head on his shoulder. His chest rises and falls with every breath, swaying me a fraction.

"Robbie told me you're leaving."

I nod, chewing my lip.

"Good for you. You'll go far."

They're kind words, but not the ones I want. I screw my eyes shut against the tears brimming there.

"Is that all?"

Aleksi huffs out a laugh. "I'd come with you if you let me, but I don't think you will."

I'm already shaking my head.

"Robbie needs you here."

We finish the bottle together, passing it back and forth, until there's nothing left to do with our hands. Then I turn and slide onto Aleksi's lap, toying with the soft ends of his hair.

His kiss sends heat scorching through my chilled body, from the top of my head to my toes in my boots. I trace my thumbs along his jawline and kiss him back, pouring all the things I can't make myself say into the motion.

We undress each other slowly, both keeping our tops on against the cold. I kick the onesie off my ankles and tug my leggings down too, then pull my panties to the side.

Aleksi tears the condom packet open, nearly losing it to the wind, and I break down in giggles as he slides it on.

When I sink down onto his cock, it's like coming home. My chest cracks open.

We rock together, the carriage swaying with our movements, but it's gentle. Slow. Neither of us wants it to end, so we drag it out until our nerves sing. Finally, when we can't put it off any longer, Aleksi reaches between us and rubs at my clit. I rock faster and faster, the pressure building, until my orgasm thunders through me and I shatter.

Aleksi follows close behind, his lips pressed to my temple. He grunts like it's dredged from the depths of his soul, his arms clutching me so tight I can hardly breathe.

Afterwards, bundled back in our clothes, I sit in his lap.

"Robbie thinks you're coming back."
I sigh and kiss Aleksi's cheek.
"I'm not."

Chapter 14

ONE YEAR LATER

I step one foot back in the carnival and thank God I'm home. The sea of tents and stalls stretches as far as the eye can see, bigger than any single circus—even Cirque de la Lune. Flames leap against the night sky, spewing from the tossed-back mouths of fire eaters. Nuts crackle in roasting pans, their scent lacing the air and making my stomach rumble.

Four days, I lasted in Ohio this time. A new record since my career took off.

Whatever. I finally have an excuse not to visit so much. With my name on towering billboards by the roadside, and topping the list of acts on carnival flyers, Hazel Harris is busy. In demand.

The carnival grounds are so massive that it's basically a tent city. There are recognizable boroughs as I wander through the alleys—clusters of fortune tellers and palm readers; a clearing filled with belly dancers and stilt-walkers; a food district heady with curry spices and the sizzle of roasting pork.

Music plays from all directions, sometimes coming together to harmonize and riff off each other, other times competing in loud, clashing battles. Drums pound and strings twang. It's urgent, alive.

I breathe in deeply, soaking up the chaos. The swirl of colors and bustle of the crowd. These aren't even the audiences—these are the workers and performers of all the country's biggest carnivals, coming together to posture and perform. To drink, fight and fuck.

Some things never change.

Feather-light fingers dance along my hair, and I slap the pickpocket away without looking. A gangly teenager hurries past, his hands shoved in his pockets. A dark flush tints the top of his ears.

Yeah. He should know better than to try his luck on a carnie.

"Hazel!"

A few people recognize me as I weave through the stands, a duffel bag slung on my shoulder. I nod back, offering a slight smile but not stopping to talk. Some of them, I've met. Some of them are complete strangers.

It happens. I've made a name for myself in the last year. Plus, I'm pretty easy to spot, with my signature purple hair.

"Are you too good to catch up with an old friend, girl?"

A voice cuts through the rabble, and I freeze, chest suddenly tight. I whip my head around, looking for the source, and my face cracks into a wide smile when I spot Ginny at her hot dog stall.

They're here, then. Robbie's workers. Cirque de la Lune.

I had wondered. Just once or twice.

"Ginny!" I elbow my way through the crowd, dumping my bag at her feet to throw my arms around her neck. She's bonier since the last time we hugged, and the thought makes me cling on tighter.

"You fell off the map," Ginny scolds, pulling back to grip my shoulders with gnarled fingers.

I shrug, uneasy. "It's no secret where I've been working."

She shakes me, fingers digging in. "What good is that if you never call?"

I grimace. Ginny's right. I know she is. I've wanted to reach out for months, but something kept holding me back. I typed out texts to Danika, then deleted them; hand-wrote letters to Kamran, then screwed them into a ball.

I left without really saying goodbye. And I didn't keep in touch, even though I missed them all every day.

Why should they want to hear from me now?

"I'm sorry. I had to figure some stuff out."

Ginny squints at my face, her old eyes a paler blue than before. Her mouth twists like she's sucking on a boiled candy, her crimson lipstick stark against her white skin.

Then she gives a sharp nod, and I can breathe again.

"It's good to see you, Hazel."

"You too."

We exchange brief updates and promise to find each other later. Ginny tells me about the moonshine she's been brewing in an old pewter bathtub and offers me a bottle if I swing by her trailer.

I don't ask her about the guys. Kamran, Robbie and Aleksi. If they're still hurting, I'll hate myself, and if they're not, I don't want to hear that either.

When I finally scoop up my duffel bag from the dirt, I'm hit with a sudden sense of deja vu.

Like I've been here before. Like I've always been coming here.

The feeling clings to me like cobwebs as I make my way deeper into the heart of the carnival. As a headliner—one of only three, picked out of every circus in the country—I've got a Bedouin tent all to myself in the heart of the action. I follow the directions scrawled in pen on the back of my hand, poking my head into three wrong doorways before I finally find the right one.

It's the size of my old trailer; a rectangular tent made from dark grey canvas. When I unfasten one side of the door and slip inside, I'm met with glowing bulbs hanging from the ceiling. They fill the space with a warm glow and cast shadows on the floor.

There's a double bed, slung low to the ground, covered in pillows and blankets. Mismatched rugs cover every inch of the tent floor, overlapping at weird angles.

Four giant cushions cluster around a tea-stand. Someone's boiled the water recently, wisps of steam curling out of the teapot. It's a masterpiece of coziness.

I think of Kamran, and my heart throbs.

A year. An entire year without seeing him, and still he's vivid in my mind's eye. I remember everything in perfect detail, from the dark hairs dusting his muscled chest to the smoky smell of his skin.

I've made it. I did what I set out to do. I made a name for myself on the trapeze, built a career out of the depths Yan left me in.

But in this moment, as grief and longing wrack my body in waves, I fantasize about how things might have been if I never left. If I stayed with the three of them and let whatever was building between us become something real.

I sling my duffel onto the bed and straighten my shoulders.

No point chasing memories.

I have a performance to give.

* * *

Tomorrow night, we'll do this show for a crowd of thousands. Tonight, though, is much more nerve-wracking. Tonight, we perform for each other.

Every performer worth their salt in the country is here. This is a chance to make a statement, to push boundaries and show what we can do.

I nearly fell off my chair when Jethro, my current boss, told me I'd been chosen to headline. I knew my routines were making waves, shaking up the trapeze scene, but I hadn't set out to be shocking. I was just telling stories.

For my performance tonight, Jethro commissioned a huge set piece. He'd raised his craggy eyebrows when I told him what I wanted, but I placed my hand on his forearm.

"Trust me. Okay?"

And he did. Why wouldn't he? I hadn't gone wrong once since he took me on a year ago. The crowds loved me, and the more adventurous theatre critics made me their darling.

And tonight, I wanted to make a splash.

Literally.

I watch the roadies roll my set into place with nerves gnawing at my stomach. A giant black satin cloth covers it from view—that should keep the crowd guessing—but I'm still worried it's all too obvious. That I'm not as visionary as I think.

There are three platforms in the big top tent—such a cavernous space that you have to crane your neck back to see the highest point. One is set up for my trapeze routine. One has a series of metal rectangles dangling overhead, like a shower of art frames. And one has two white silks falling in perfect columns.

Aleksi.

I gnaw my fingernails down to the quick all the way back to my tent. Midnight nears, and as soon as it arrives, I'll step out on that stage. The guys will see me for the first time in a year, even if I don't see them.

Will they even come to watch? Do they want to see me at all?

Unanswerable questions swirl around my brain as I duck back inside my tent. My costume hangs from a rail against the canvas wall, the feathers glossy and the jewels glinting. As soon as I lay eyes on it, my stomach lurches, and I wheel around to my mirror and dressing table.

Make-up first. One thing at a time.

Breathe.

I paint my face ghostly white, the circular motions of the sponge oddly soothing. When I line my eyes with thick black kohl, I push away thoughts of Kamran and focus on the task.

Come on, Hazel. Get it together.

For months, I've been fine, keeping their memories at bay apart from stolen moments of longing in my room. Being here, knowing they're somewhere close by…

Fire sizzles in my veins.

Once my face is painted, I lean back and inspect myself in the mirror. My eyes look huge, spiky false eyelashes brushing my cheeks. My lips are blood-red, and two black trails run down each cheek.

I look like the ultimate circus freak. Perfect.

My costume goes on easily: a black leotard crusted with dark sequins that glint emerald and blue when they catch the light. Over the top, I slip the straps for two wings over my shoulders.

Black feathers cascade down my back and tickle at my ankles.

Show time.

I don't bother trying to cover up on my walk to the tent. These wings are damn near impossible to hide, so I stride through the crowd in full view. Wolf whistles cut through the hubbub, but I keep my head locked straight. When I reach the big top, I veer away from the entrance and walk around the outside.

Some habits are hard to break. And besides, I don't want to stay in that burning crush of bodies. They'll melt my make-up and rumple my wings, for a start.

My fingers drag along the canvas, searching for a slit in the walls. My wrist twinges from the motion, but I grit my teeth and ignore it.

It'll never fully heal, but I've learned to work with it. It's an added challenge when I choreograph my routines.

My fingertips catch on a gap in the canvas, and I peel it wide enough to duck through. I have to turn sideways, shuffling so that my wings don't get caught, but when I spill through the gap, I'm in the shadows at the rear of the tent. I take a moment to soak in the crowd's roar, the muggy heat from all those bodies.

I check my palms—perfectly dry.

I've got this.

My platform is to the left of center, and I wander across to it. My mystery set is still draped in black-satin, standing proud at eight feet tall with a trapeze dangling above. Drums pound as I near the steps, so I walk straight onto the stage. Fire bursts on the front corners of the platform, and I step into the spotlight.

The drums stop. A hush falls over the crowd. I grip a handful of black satin and toss the cover into the crowd. A giant goblet stands on the platform, water sparkling through its clear glass bowl. A murmur breaks through the audience as they put the scene together.

A bird bath. I got the idea a few months ago in my parents' garden in Ohio.

I guess those visits weren't a complete waste of time.

The drums creep in again, building into a rhythm. Electric guitar reverberates through the tent from the live band on their own stage. I climb the steps at the back of the goblet, balancing on my toes on the brim.

My hands wrap around the trapeze bar, dusted with chalk. It's like easing into an armchair you've had for years; running your fingers over a favorite old book. Like coming home. Closing my eyes for a second against the dazzling spotlight, I launch myself into the air.

It's a gorgeous routine. I knew it was special as I created it. I start in my full bird costume, perched on the trapeze bar. I dance through a series of static poses, the bar barely moving an inch as I flow up, around, and below it.

Then the drums thump louder, and I start to swing. Pushing the bar higher and higher, I flip and twirl above the platform, my feathers fluttering in the breeze. My wings scrape against the trapeze cables, but it doesn't matter. All eyes are on me.

As the music darkens, becomes more sensual, the arc of the bar slows. I keep dancing and spinning around the bar until it settles over the goblet again.

Then I lower myself, slow and controlled, dangling my toes in the water.

Thousands of faces watch, rapt, as I drop into the goblet. I twirl, my wings dragging in the water, and sparkling droplets shower over the sides. Cupping the water between my palms,

I tip it over my head, shaking out my hair.

My wings are the first to come off. I drop them, sodden, over the rim. Then I dunk my head for real, flipping my hair back so that water sprays in a great arc. I keep dancing, my movements languid, as I peel the fake eyelashes from each eye. I meet the gaze of a man in the front row and flick them onto the stage.

My hands are wet as I reach for the bar again, hauling myself out of the water. I urge the trapeze to swing again, soaking wet with glistening limbs. I slide and flip and roll around the bar, spraying water droplets like diamonds.

When the music ends and I come to a stop, balancing on my toes on the goblet's rim, silence stretches taut through the crowd for the space of a breath.

Then they erupt.

The noise thunders through the tent, battering at my eardrums. I grin and bow, scanning the few faces I can see through the glare of the spotlight.

It's not them. I keep the smile fixed on my face and climb down as the next set begins.

* * *

"That was incredible."

A familiar voice cuts through my tent, and I pause as I tie my robe. I watched the other headliners, heart aching as Aleksi soared overhead, but I ducked out of the slit in the canvas as smaller acts took to the stages. They're talented too, no doubt about it, but I'm soaked through and it's November. My teeth were chattering as I toweled off.

I turn to the man standing in the center of my rugs.

"I didn't invite you in."

Yan smiles, his face full of easy charm. His shoulders are relaxed, like he has a right to be here. I hold his gaze as I inch backwards to the make-up counter.

"It's wonderful to see you, too, Hazelnut."

Ugh. He never called me that before. He must have heard Kamran say it once, and latched on.

Behind my back, I slide a palette knife into my fist. I don't care if we used to date. No man invades my space uninvited.

"Take the fucking hint, Yan."

He steps forward, ignoring me. I'm suddenly aware of my bare thighs beneath my robe, of the fact that every person for miles around is currently crammed in that big top tent.

"I have a proposition."

"Not interested."

He grins, eyes slightly manic. "You haven't heard it yet."

"I don't need to."

Was he always such a fucking creep? My pulse thumps in my ears as I skirt around the edge of the tent. I grip the palette knife hard in my hand, suddenly glad for the answering twinge in my wrist. It centers me, brings me back to myself.

I plant my feet and raise my chin.

Yan smiles, an unhealthy sheen of sweat on his face.

"I've thought about it, and I think we're ready to be partners again. We've both made names for ourselves as solo performers, and as a double act we'd take the circus world by storm."

The name I've made is far more famous than Yan's. I guess that's why he's so off-kilter, his tongue darting out to wet his lips.

I don't know what's happened to him over the last year, and frankly, I don't care. But I get the sense that things have gone downhill for Yan since he dropped Sasha Daniels.

He's a few feet away, brown eyes fixed on mine. I hold out a palm as he moves to step closer.

"Hard pass, Yan. Go and find someone you haven't dropped, insulted and abandoned."

He opens his mouth to argue, but I cut him off.

"I'm done talking. Get out."

Yan stays rooted in place, his chest heaving.

"You need me," he begins, his voice ragged. "You need me more than I need you—"

"Prove it." I jerk my chin at the doorway. "I'll shake your hand if it turns out you're right."

Yan sucks in a deep breath, fury clouding his features before he smooths his face back to a mask.

"Hazel," he murmurs, reaching for me, and I hold up my knife.

"Get. Out."

He jerks forward, rage contorting his face, and I slash out wildly. Yan stumbles back, hand clapped to his cheek as beads of blood roll down his skin.

"You bitch," he breathes, staring down at the blood on his fingers. He lunges forward, coming for me again, when a shout knocks him off balance.

I kick that psycho in the crotch with every ounce of strength I have. Yan collapses to the rug, winded and groaning, his face sickly white.

Robbie strides across the tent and takes my face in his hands, blue eyes darting over my body.

"Are you okay? Did he hurt you? If he laid a finger on you—"

I place a hand on his forearm. "I handled it."

Robbie grits his teeth but nods, gaze raking over me again

in case I'm lying. I stare at him, heart slamming against my rib cage. He's here.

A year. It's been an entire year since I saw his face. Robbie looks tired, his cheekbones sharper, but he's still the same. Still heartbreakingly beautiful.

I can see the moment he comes back to himself. When he remembers we're almost strangers to each other now, and he goes to withdraw his hands.

"Don't." I tangle my fingers in his sleeve, clutching him closer. "Not yet."

Robbie lets out a shaky sigh and steps closer, thumbs stroking my cheeks. I bite my bottom lip, my eyes dropping to his mouth, and lean in.

A burbling groan rises up from the rug, bringing us crashing back to reality. We step apart, cheeks flushed, and Robbie glares down at the crumpled Yan with disgust.

"I'll take care of him."

He grabs Yan by the back of the collar and drags him to the doorway. I watch them both go, wrapping my arms tight around my middle.

"Robbie?"

He pauses, glancing back over his shoulder, one foot on my rugs and one on the grass outside.

"Come find me after."

His mouth twitches, and he nods, a sparkle in his blue eyes.

Chapter 15

The flames gutter in the fire pit, whipped away by the wind. I rest the soles of my boots on the iron rim, groaning as the heat licks up my legs. I've been frozen since the water from my show cooled on me as I watched Aleksi perform.

"You'll melt your boots."

Danika elbows me, smirking as she tips back the whiskey. A bottle of Ginny's moonshine rests abandoned on the grass between our lawn chairs. I'm surprised it doesn't burn straight through the glass—when we sniffed at the opening, tears streamed down both our cheeks.

Not tonight. I'm riding the high of the show, and the thrill of kicking Yan's ass. I don't want to ruin the mood via accidental liver damage.

I grin but don't move my boots away. "Their sacrifice is noted."

Finally, hours after the end of the show, my limbs are warming up. Wedged between Danika and one of the other roadies, and with the flames licking at the bottom of my shoes, the icy numbness in my bones has started to recede.

I glance around the gathered chairs and the heads of people walking past. I'm getting a crick in my neck, I've been looking for Robbie so much.

He said he'd come find me, but he's nowhere to be seen. What if that was it—my only chance to see him again? We barely said anything. There's so much I want to tell him.

There are questions, too, weighing down my tongue. Like whether he and Kamran are still... involved. Like whether Sasha is earning her role on the trapeze.

I won't ask those, even if he comes back. No matter how much I'm dying to.

"Stop your staring, Jesus Christ. He's there—look."

Danika points at a figure cutting through the crowds, making a beeline towards us. But it's not Robbie that elbows his way to our side—it's Aleksi.

"Are you okay?"

He barges my legs off the fire pit, kneeling in front of my chair. When his gentle brown eyes skate over my face, it's like no time has passed.

This is about Yan. Robbie must have told Aleksi what his brother did.

"I'm fine."

All my bravado from earlier has fled, and I'm suddenly shy. I smile at the acrobat kneeling at my feet, and tuck a strand of his hair behind one ear.

Aleksi sucks in a breath, his eyes fluttering closed. At once, it's all those months ago, and we're huddled together in that Ferris wheel. The wind howls against the open carriage door, and we cling together like shipwreck survivors.

Aleksi opens his eyes, and reality floods back in. It's been a year. We haven't spoken. He could have a girlfriend, for all I know. I snatch my hand back, fiddling with the locket around my neck.

"You should talk to him," Aleksi says, his gaze locked on my necklace. He's not talking about his asshole brother.

"Where is he?"

Aleksi pushes off his thighs and rises to his feet. His face is shadowed, back-lit by the fire when he offers his hand.

"I'll show you."

I place my fingers in his.

* * *

Kamran holds court among a circle of fire eaters, breathing flames at the sky. He tosses his head back and laughs between tricks, lines of sweat sliding down his bare chest. His black pants hang low on his narrow hips, the muscles pointing the way inside.

Has he not fucking noticed it's November? I clench my chilled hands in the sleeves of my sweatshirt as Aleksi leads me into the clearing between tents. For a crazy moment, I want to yell at Kamran to put some damn layers on.

I bite back the words. He's not mine to worry over. Out of all of them, he must hate me the most. When I left Cirque de la Lune a year ago, the goodbyes crushed my chest until I couldn't breathe. Leaving Aleksi after the Ferris wheel was bad enough; hugging Ginny and Danika goodbye had me weeping.

I couldn't bring myself to see Kamran one last time. It hurt too much.

But I know when he turns his cold eyes on me that I deserve his sneer of disdain. I took the coward's way out, and after all we'd become to each other, I left him without a word of goodbye.

"Hi," I croak, fighting a wince when his amber eyes narrow.

Kamran leaves the circle of fire-eaters, prowling towards me and Aleksi. I glance at my guide, but he can't help me with this. It's my mess to clear up.

"Look who deigned to visit." Kamran comes to a stop a few feet away. His kohl is smeared over his cheekbones, his curls tangled and wild. "What can I do for you, Harris?"

I've never wanted to be called Hazelnut more in my whole damn life. I hate that stupid name with a passion, but somewhere along the way, I grew to love it from Kamran.

I cut to the chase. Kamran is flighty at the best of times, and I'm not sure how many minutes he'll allow me.

"I'm sorry." A few heads turn to eavesdrop, but I rush on. "I shouldn't have left like that. I was a coward."

Kamran cocks his head to one side, regarding me. After a second, he rolls his eyes and turns to glare over his shoulder.

The other fire-eaters huddle away, muttering to each other.

"You told Robbie you were leaving, correct?" he says when he faces me again. "And you spent your last night with Aleksi."

The man in question shifts next to me, but says nothing.

I pause, then bite my lip and nod. Kamran's face shutters, and he moves to turn away.

"I couldn't do it," I blurt out. "I knew if I saw you again, I'd stay." I swallow, my throat tight. "Please, Kamran."

Aleksi murmurs something and turns on his heel, walking back the way we came. I'm left in the shadows on the outskirts of the clearing, Kamran watching me with unreadable eyes.

"It wasn't..." He speaks slowly, choosing his words with care. "It wasn't that you cared for them more?"

I shake my head so hard I twinge my neck.

"I couldn't bear leaving you." I lick my lips, and go all-in. "I still can't bear it. I left my heart with you three."

Kamran inhales through his nose, tilting his head back to look at the stars. When he drops his chin, his amber eyes burn in the shadows, and a smirk tugs at his lips.

"Well, you know what they say. No safer hiding place than with a thief."

* * *

We collect Aleksi on the way back to the fire pits. He leans against a closed popcorn stand, his arms crossed and his eyes fixed on the path to the clearing.

It's hard to tell for sure in the dark, but I think he relaxes when he sees our joined hands.

"Thank God for that," he mutters as we reach him, pushing upright. He falls into step beside us as we wind through the alleys, matching our strides. I can't tell up from down, I'm so dizzied to find myself walking between them again. But one of them must know where we're going, because we emerge on the edge of the crowd.

Aleksi takes my other hand as we walk, his thumb rubbing over my pulse point.

"You were beautiful," he leans in to murmur in my ear. "You stole the show."

Aleksi doesn't exaggerate, and I blush with fierce pride. He always saw my potential. Even when no one else did.

I'm glad not to let him down. To show him he was right after all. It's always Aleksi I see in my mind's eye when I craft a routine. It's him I want to impress and seduce; him I want clapping for me.

We round the fire pits, and the feeling of deja vu hits me again. I half expect Robbie to stand on an upturned barrel and hold court, giving a show report.

He doesn't do that. My old boss isn't even here. My heart sinks in my chest like a stone as I stare around all the wrong faces. Danika winks when she catches my eye, raising her eyebrows at the two hands joined in mine. I force a smile and keep looking, peering into every nook and shadow.

"He's not here," I say at last, my shoulders slumping.

Kamran squeezes my fingers, his voice bitter in my ear.

"Robbie has never known what he wanted. Don't take it personally, Hazelnut."

I nod, squeezing his hand back, and let them lead me away from the fire pits. My tent isn't far, just a short walk away, and my palms grow clammy with nerves as we approach.

"It doesn't matter," I turn to tell them on the threshold. I try to believe it myself. "Robbie never really wanted me like that."

I pull the tent flap open and freeze.

"Yes, I did."

My old boss sits on the bed, and pushes to his feet when I enter. Aleksi and Kamran file in behind me, their warmth reassuring at my back.

Fuck. He still draws me like a magnet. I didn't get a proper look at him earlier, not with Yan gasping for breath on my rug. I take him in with greedy eyes, desperate to absorb every detail. His blond hair, curling around his ears; the scruff on his jaw. Robbie's dressed in black like always, a tool belt slung around his hips, and his chest is even broader than I remembered. It heaves as he takes in a breath, his eyes flicking between Kamran and I.

None of us say anything. The silence stretches on. Finally, Aleksi huffs a quiet laugh and slips out from behind me.

"I'll make the tea."

Chapter 16

A year ago, I'd have chopped my right leg off to get these three men in my bedroom.

Well, maybe not a leg. I need that for trapeze. But a toe or something.

Now they're here, though, I don't know what to do with myself. I'm like a puppet with its strings snipped: clumsy with my gestures and wooden as I step into the tent.

"Um. Tea, yeah. Sit down, guys."

I wave a jerky hand at the floor cushions clustered around the tea station. Aleksi's already there, kneeling over the teapot, an amused smile tugging his lips.

It's all right for him. He's not hosting a summit for a one time would-be orgy.

"Shut up," I hiss as I lower myself to sit cross-legged beside him.

"I didn't say anything," Aleksi murmurs back, face serene.

Honestly, screw this guy.

That's the idea, my frazzled brain whispers, and a manic bubble expands in my chest. Laughter crowds up my throat, and I swallow it back. What the hell am I doing? I am not the sort of person to declare love for one guy, let alone three. It's left me exposed and raw, my fight-or-flight instincts kicking in.

Kamran's palm rests lightly on my knee, and my racing heartbeat slows a little. I pull a deep breath into my lungs and let it go, turning to give him a quick smile. He lounges catlike on the cushion, looking for all the world like the centerfold in a magazine.

I glance at Robbie and catch him staring, his blue eyes exhausted and sad. Something tells me these guys have not been getting along since I left.

A tiny, petty part of myself rejoices in that idea. Not that I want them miserable, but I've been twisted up with jealousy at the thought of them happy without me there.

I know. I'm the worst. But I can't help how I feel.

"So…" I lick my lips. "How have things been?"

Kamran scoffs. "Must we make awkward chit chat?"

His gaze cuts to me, and I watch as heat darkens those amber eyes. He inches closer, enveloping me with his delicious smoky scent.

"You've got some atoning to do, Hazelnut. And I don't know about these two, but I have some ideas."

Robbie clears his throat.

"She's not the only one who needs to atone."

He frowns at me from the cushion opposite, stroking a hand along his jaw. The radio crackles on his belt and he curses, switching it off and throwing it onto the rug.

"Still on duty?" I ask. I figured here, at least, at this massive gathering, Robbie would finally get some time off.

Robbie shrugs, his face guilty, and Aleksi snorts.

"Robbie's the organizer, Hazel. He brought dozens of circuses together from all over the country, just to see you again."

My old boss flushes crimson, staring with sudden fascination at the teapot. I blink at him, running over all the times in my mind when he threatened to fire me or send me away. I knew he was attracted to me, sure—Robbie's a blusher, and I'm not blind—but he always seemed so keen to get rid of me. Like wanting me was a punishment, or a chore.

I clear my throat. "I don't understand. You wanted me gone, Robbie."

He looks up, eyes hard, hand clenching into a fist on his knee. "Never, Hazel. I never wanted that."

Kamran sighs, stretching until his spine pops. "What you have to understand about Robbie here is that feelings scare the shit out of him. He'd rather push someone away than give something real a chance." He smirks nastily at Robbie. "Isn't that right, boss man?"

Robbie grits his teeth but holds Kamran's gaze.

Finally, he speaks, voice low. "That's right."

* * *

The whistle of steam cuts through the tent, making us all jump. Aleksi takes the teapot off the heat, sliding a wire cage of tea leaves into the water to brew.

We all watch like it's the most fascinating documentary we've ever seen.

It's that, or meet each other's eyes.

Finally, I can't stand it any longer. Talking about feelings has never been my strong suit—I'm like Robbie that way. I'd rather show how I feel, and be shown back. Actions speak louder than words.

Decision made, I turn on my cushion, push onto my knees,

175

and swing a leg over Kamran's lap. His hands immediately fall to my hips, gripping tight and pulling me close.

I rub the tip of my nose against his, my hands cradling his jaw.

"Are we okay?" I murmur, just for us. He smiles, his eyes crinkling.

"Always," he whispers back, lunging up to seal his mouth to mine. I kiss him like I'm starved for him, scrabbling at his shoulders. Kamran's hands slide up my back to tangle in my hair, and I moan at the feeling of his fingers scratching my scalp.

When I'm getting dizzy from lack of oxygen, we break apart, chests heaving. Kamran plucks at the woolen sleeve of my sweater.

"It's weird doing this without the onesie."

I snort and punch him lightly on the shoulder before clambering upright. When I turn to Robbie, his pupils are blown wide and his face is etched with longing.

For me. For Kamran. Us together; us apart.

"You're not my boss anymore," I tease as I slide onto his lap. Robbie's arms come up to cage me in—like I'd ever want to leave.

"Thank God."

"Oh, I don't know." I stroke my fingertips over his scruff. "I thought it was sexy."

"Agreed," Kamran puts in behind me, and Robbie shoots him an exasperated look over my shoulder.

"Play nice," I whisper, leaning in to nibble on his bottom lip. Robbie groans, a tortured sound, and winds his arms around me tighter. "You want him just as badly. Don't pretend."

"I can't have favorites," he grinds out, his Scottish accent getting thicker the more wound up he is. Still, his eyes flick to Kamran before they seal back on me.

"Robbie." I take a fistful of his sweater and shake it. "Seriously. Who gives a fuck?"

He stares at me, jaw tight, emotions flickering over his face. I can see the exact moment he gives in, his shoulders slumping.

"Probably no one." His mouth twists. "I should never have chased you out."

I shrug, far more casual about it with the echo of applause ringing in my ears.

"I'm glad you did. And now it means I can do this."

I grind down against his cock, rock hard in his jeans. He grips my hips, thrusting up to meet me, and turns his head to bite at my neck. Heat roars through my body as my pulse thunders in my ears, and even though I hear the other guys breathing, only Robbie and I exist in this moment.

His touch is rough, his kiss biting. All that frustration he carries around in his tense shoulders, he unleashes on me now.

Robbie winds his hand around my hair and tugs. I gasp, and my pussy throbs in response.

"Forget the fucking tea."

Distantly, I hear Kamran and Aleksi bickering. But every ounce of my focus narrows down to Robbie's hands, his tongue, his cock.

"Get this off." I tug at his sweater. I want to see him. I've never really seen him.

Robbie clicks his tongue as he pulls the sweater over his head and tosses it onto the rug. He smirks at me, grabbing my hips and grinding me against him.

"Don't forget who's in charge here, Hazel."

I lick a stripe up his neck. "Prove it."

177

His hand flashes out, smacking my ass cheek, and I moan, my pussy flooding. I rock against him faster, desperate for friction, but Robbie gathers me and drops me on the rug. When he kneels, the zipper of his jeans is level with my nose.

"Are you all talk, Hazel?" His voice is ragged. He winds a hand into my hair and tugs me close. "Show me what you can do."

My pussy throbs again, and I yank his zipper down, flicking his button undone with trembling fingers. I work his jeans and boxers down around his hips. Robbie watches my every movement with searing eyes.

His cock is warm and heavy in my palm. My mouth waters as I stroke it from tip to base, the velvet skin sliding. The scent of soap and salt fills my nose.

I lean forward, lips opening, then pause, a thought crossing my mind.

Robbie grunts, impatient, but I glance over my shoulder at Kamran.

"Want to help?"

Kamran's watching us with hungry eyes, and he twitches forwards at my offer. But he clenches his jaw and settles back on his cushion, raising his eyebrows at Robbie.

"Well?" he asks, voice hard.

Robbie sucks in a breath.

"Yes. You too, Kamran."

"I'm fine over here," Aleksi puts in, and I smirk at him as Kamran crawls over. He settles next to me, reaching for Robbie too, but a voice stills him.

"Wait. Not yet."

Kamran glances up, hurt clouding his eyes, but Robbie rubs a thumb along his sharp jaw.

"Come here." He tugs Kamran to kneel, and slides that palm around his neck. It's the same way he touched him all those months ago in Kamran's trailer, as I sat in his lap and held my breath so I wouldn't break the spell.

Kamran reaches down with one hand and tangles his fingers through mine. Robbie's other hand tightens in my hair.

Their mouths slam together like waves crashing onto rocks. It's been so long for these two, so bittersweet, and everything they can't say in words, they pour into this kiss. My heart hammers in my chest as I watch them, and I might have drawn away, except they hold me tight in place.

A feather light touch over my shoulder blades makes me jerk in surprise. Aleksi settles behind me, one knee on either side of my hips.

"This is perfect," he murmurs against my skin, kissing up the side of my neck. "More Hazel for me."

I sigh and lean back against him, his warmth flooding over my back.

"I feel like we should leave them to it," I mutter under my breath.

"Don't you dare."

Two pairs of eyes glare down at me, their mouths set in matching frowns. Kamran's fingers tighten around mine, and Robbie rubs his thumb along my scalp.

"It doesn't work without you, Hazel." Kamran's smile is rueful. "It all falls apart."

He glances at Robbie then settles back at my side, scorching me with a kiss before raising our linked hands to Robbie's cock.

"Now let's blow this repressed idiot's mind."

* * *

I've always freaking loved blow jobs. I hardly admit it to anyone, because hey, I'm not looking for offers. But nothing makes me wetter than working my mouth on a cock, using my tongue and lips and hands to suck the soul clean out of someone's body.

In Kamran, I've found a kindred spirit. He attacks the task like his life depends on it, his eyelashes dark against his hollowed cheeks. We take it in turns to suck Robbie down, lips stretched around him, then lick along one side each before meeting at the tip.

We break away to kiss each other, panting into each other's mouths.

"You're killing me," Robbie grits out, his thigh muscle twitching under my palm. "You have the attention span of two gnats."

I break away, raising my eyebrows at Kamran. He nods.

We turn on Robbie like avenging demons. Kamran swallows him down in one go while I suck a bruise into Robbie's hip, fingernails scratching down his inner thigh. Robbie curses overhead, his hands gripping tighter in our hair.

Kamran releases his cock with a pop.

"I think that's plenty of that."

Robbie splutters, but I grin and let go too. Maybe it's cruel, but I love the dark flush of Robbie's cheeks and his glazed, wide eyes.

Besides, we're just getting started. And we have a lot of time to make up for.

"Lay him out, Kam."

My partner in crime yanks Robbie down to lay on the rug.

He wrestles the rest of his clothes off, dancing out of reach when Robbie grabs for him. Aleksi tips back to rest on his palms, smirking, his long hair sliding over his shoulder.

"Try to leave him vaguely in one piece, you two. I hear Scottish grannies are vengeful."

"No promises." I stand, pulling my clothes over my head and tugging my leggings down my thighs. I glance around and find three sets of eyes glued to my every move.

I go slower, teasing my panties down my hips. Three groans echo through the tent and I smirk, kicking them off my ankles.

"You're behind." I point at Aleksi and Kamran. "Get naked."

Then I straddle Robbie's hips and drop to my knees, facing towards his feet.

"Condom," I snap out, and someone thrusts one into my open palm. I tear the packet open and roll it over Robbie's cock. His stomach shudders under my ass, and I squirm against him, giving him another tug.

Robbie pushes onto his elbows and rakes his fingers through my hair.

"Gorgeous," he mutters, almost to himself. "You're so beautiful I can't stand it."

I line his cock up with my entrance just as Aleksi kneels over Robbie's legs right in front of me. He's naked, all that flawless skin soft in the lantern light, and I reach out to grab his shoulders.

Aleksi takes my hips and guides me down, all the way to the base. My pussy stretches around Robbie's cock, a whimper escaping my lips.

"That's it," Aleksi says as I rock my hips. "Show him who's really boss, sweetheart."

Kamran kneels at my side, running his hands over my bare

181

skin. He kisses my neck as Aleksi urges me faster, his grip tight on my hips. Behind me, Robbie groans, ragged and ruined.

It doesn't take long for the pressure to build in my core, winding taut until I could scream for relief. I slam down harder on Robbie's cock, my thighs burning. Aleksi trails one finger across my stomach and down to my center. He rubs at my clit, two, three times, and I shatter, nails digging into his shoulders. My pussy clamps down on Robbie's cock, and I feel him swell inside me.

He lets out a tortured groan, spilling inside.

When I ease off Robbie's cock, my legs tremble, but the hunger still aches in my core. I flop down on the rug beside Robbie, pulling Aleksi with me as I go.

He's ready, a condom rolled on his hard cock, and he pushes inside me in one thrust.

"I missed you," he whispers into the skin of my neck, licking a bead of sweat. I whimper and nod, pushing my hips up to meet his and winding my arms around his neck.

My acrobat. He's so good. So kind. None of us deserve him, but here he is.

I crane my neck to the side and find Robbie's mouth sealed around Kamran's cock. The fire-eater winks at me, his fingers playing in Robbie's hair.

A breathy laugh escapes my lips, and I rest my head back with a thud. Aleksi moves inside me, every blissful inch of him, and the tent fills with our sighs and the whisper-slide of skin.

My chest cracks open.

I never want this to end.

We lay together afterwards in an exhausted, sticky pile, chatting about nonsense until our bodies stir and we go again.

And again.

And a few more times after that.

We come together in a wild array of combinations and positions. I lose track of which hands belong to who; which lips are nibbling my earlobe. It's everything I've wanted all this time and more, my heart singing as our bodies come together.

It's so perfect that it's almost cruel. The hours tick by, the sky paling outside the tent, and with every passing minute, reality sidles closer.

We're here for two more days, then we'll be gone again. Scattered to the wind.

* * *

"Where are you going next?"

Robbie slides a lock of my hair through his fingers, my head pillowed on his chest. On either side of us, Kamran and Aleksi sleep stretched out on my bed.

It's a tight fit, but we made it work. No way was one of us sleeping apart.

"World tour." My lips are numb as I speak. I've been so excited for this, counting down the days until we leave in a month. "We're starting in Europe. Prague first, Vienna second." I shift against him, brushing a stray hair from my mouth. "It's Italy I'm looking forward to most."

My words are excited, but by the tone of my voice you'd think I was headed to a funeral. Tonight was... everything. The best night of my life. I'd never felt so close to another human being.

And now I'm about to flit across the globe, ending our story before it's truly begun.

Robbie hums, rubbing circles on my shoulder blades.

"You deserve it, Hazel. You deserve all the good things."

Moisture burns in the back of my eyes, and I screw them shut. I won't cry and pop this bubble we're in. I won't.

Besides, what do I have to cry about? Amazing sex and a world tour, *boo hoo*?

I breathe in sharply through my nose and let it out.

"I'll miss you."

Robbie sighs. "We'll miss you, too."

We. Not I. Like they're bound together too, and when I leave they'll be missing a piece. For a crazy second, I think of offering to stay. To rejoin Robbie's circus and headline on trapeze.

The words never make it past my lips. I can't work for Robbie again. And I can't go backwards in my career, no matter how sweet the temptation.

"Where are you guys headed?"

If Robbie hears how strangled I sound, he doesn't mention it.

"Back to the mountains, I think. It's been too long."

I nod, pressing a kiss to his hard chest.

I know what he means. A year is a very long time.

Chapter 17

I sling my duffel bag onto the conveyor belt and smile blandly at the check-in worker. The airport is half-empty, mercifully quiet in these pre-dawn hours, and she stifles a yawn as she types in my details, her red mouth twisting.

"Any more luggage?"

She slaps a flight label through the handle of my bag. It looks kind of pathetic next to the glossy suitcases lined up on the belt behind it—deflated and shabby.

Whatever. You don't pack heavy in the circus.

I shake my head, extremely grateful not to need any weird personal equipment for trapeze. A few counters over, the fire-eaters and stilt-walkers are locked in a drawn out argument with the check-in worker, gesturing angrily at their bags.

"Just that."

I dig my phone out of my pocket and check the time. Hours. We have hours yet, of sitting and waiting for our plane. Then we'll sit and wait for hours more in the air before finally touching down in Europe.

I'm excited for this. I am.

It's just too damn early.

"Your gate will be announced within an hour. Enjoy your flight."

I'm not sure anyone has ever enjoyed a commercial flight, least of all in economy, but I mutter my thanks. When I step away from the line, sadness washes over me again.

Distractions. I need distractions. I can't think about what I'm leaving behind—can't let the memories of those goodbyes drown me.

"I see why you avoided this now," Kamran said, resting his forehead against mine. "I feel like someone's chopping off a limb."

I swallow and shake myself.

Coffee. It's never too early for coffee.

There's a bland, chain-store cafe squatting in the corner of the lobby. I jerk my chin at my boss, Jethro, and tilt my head at the empty tables.

"Going to fuel up," I call, and Jethro grins, his eyes twinkling. I don't know what he's so damn happy about—he's about to have a troupe of fire-eaters with no fire—but I can't bring myself to care.

It's been like this for the entire month. A hole in my chest, aching and sore, and waves of longing wracking my form.

They're probably fine. No doubt they've already moved on. Bitterness sours my mouth as I wander up to the counter.

"Latte, please. Large."

Maybe a vat of hot milk will help me sleep on the plane. Doubtful, but maybe.

The barista nods, not even raising his head. I don't blame him—if I worked here, I wouldn't bother to smile at customers either. The machine hisses and whirs, grinding beans and steaming milk, and I slide a loyalty card off the stack.

Perhaps they've moved on as a unit. Found another girl to act as their glue.

The barista clears his throat, and I blink at the card crumpled in my fist.

I pay up, cheeks flaming, but he really doesn't care. Good for him.

I grab my paper cup and wander to a table by the windows. It looks out over the car park, thousands of cars lined up in blocks like shiny beetles. A plane soars past overhead, red lights flashing on the tips of its wings.

That'll be us in a few hours. Adios, America.

I sip my latte, burning my tongue, and wince at the flavor. It's probably fine, made just right, but the rocket fuel they brew at the circus has ruined me for other drinks.

I place the cup on the sticky table and sink down in my chair.

The second I close my eyes, I see them. Robbie, his intense blue eyes searing straight to my soul. Kamran's languid stride, his catlike movements—the dusting of glitter on his golden brown chest. Aleksi's low voice calling me sweetheart as his arms wind around my waist.

The hole in my chest throbs harder, and I wince, opening my eyes. I stare out at the car park instead, desperate for a car-jacking or a breakdown. Any kind of distraction.

"Are these seats taken?"

I jerk and stare up at the three men circling my table, my heart sinking.

"Oh God. It's happened. I've actually gone mad."

Kamran chuckles, flinging himself into the chair opposite.

"Tell us something we don't know."

I frown at them and blink hard, but they don't disappear.

Holy shit. They're really here. Part of me sings with joy, but the other part wants to kick them in the teeth. They're making this departure so much harder than it needs to be.

"You didn't need to see me off…"

Their smiles drop when they see my frown. Robbie clears his throat and strokes a finger over my hand where it rests on the table.

"Do you not want us here, Hazel?"

My heart squeezes in my chest. I shake my head quickly.

"Of course not. I mean, of course I do." I lurch out of my chair, throwing my arms around his neck. I breathe him in, calm spreading through my veins. I can't believe he's here.

Kamran grunts, and I glance back to see him mopping up spilled latte with paper napkins. He catches my eye and holds up a palm.

"Carry on. I'm used to doing all the work. Wouldn't want Aleksi here to break a nail."

Aleksi rolls his eyes but snatches up a napkin, dabbing at the mess I made. Robbie's shoulders shake with laughter under my arms, and I turn back to him.

"I can't believe you came all this way just to say goodbye."

His eyes tighten, and he shifts his weight between his feet.

"That's, ah… not exactly why we're here."

I rock back onto my heels, letting go of Robbie so I can see all three of them. They look tense, matching guilty expressions on their faces.

"For fuck's sake," I mutter. Then, louder: "What have you done?"

"They sold their souls," a voice calls from behind us. I spin around to find Jethro grinning by the coffee shop rail. My new boss clicks his tongue, a pat of tobacco tucked in his cheek. He's the opposite of Robbie in every way: cheery instead of reticent, dark and bristly instead of blond. He's in his fifties, his skin weathered and lined, and he winks at me when he catches my eye.

"I don't…" I look helplessly at Aleksi. "I don't understand."

"Robbie sold Cirque de la Lune. Passed it on to someone else." Aleksi steps to my side, a gentle hand gripping my elbow. "We've joined Jethro's line-up. All three of us."

I shoot Robbie a confused look, and he gives me a wry smile. "I won't be on stage. Jethro needed a right-hand man."

"Okay…" I mutter, nodding slowly. "Okay."

My pulse is racing again, and I lean a palm on the sticky table.

"We don't have to come," Aleksi urges me, running his hand up to grip my shoulder. "Only if you want us to. Hazel. Look at me."

His brown eyes are narrowed and clear. I take a deep breath, grabbing a fistful of his shirt.

"Come with us." My lips are numb, and my head spins. "Yes. Please come with me."

The tension creasing his brow melts away, and Aleksi gathers me into his arms.

"We couldn't stand you leaving again," he whispers into my hair.

I nod, my chin scraping his collarbone.

"Neither could I."

* * *

The seat belt light dings off, and up ahead, three people race for the plane toilet. I unclip my belt, wriggling in my seat, my ass already going numb.

At least I fit in the chair. Next to me on either side, Aleksi and Robbie are practically folded in half, their shoulders brushing mine. The person sitting in front of Aleksi shoves their seat back with a jolt, and Aleksi grunts as the in-flight magazine jabs into his knee. He glares straight ahead, his nose inches from the TV screen mounted on the back of the chair.

I nudge Robbie with my elbow.

"This is where your whole big, burly, alpha male thing really backfires."

He snorts, shifting in his seat, trying and failing to fit his legs comfortably.

"It's not like we grew this big on purpose."

I find the 'Recline' button on his armrest and press it, jolting him back. A voice pipes up behind us.

"Fucking hilarious."

Kamran's head pops up behind Robbie's chair, hair rumpled and eyes already bleary from sleep. For as long as I've known him, Kamran's ability to fall asleep in seconds has been legendary. There were faint snores drifting from his row before the air stewards were done pointing out emergency exits.

"Sorry," Robbie grunts, in a voice that says he does not give a shit.

Kamran grumbles, but presses a kiss to the top of Robbie's head before he drops back down out of sight.

"I thought he'd feel left out sitting back there on his own, but he's won the lotto." I jerk my head towards the row. "Two empty seats."

Robbie huffs and prods at his TV screen. I bite my lip.

"You can go back there if you want. You'll have more space."

Robbie levels me a look that makes my toes curl, even in the stuffy airplane cab.

"I've had a month's worth of Kamran Lajani. You're not getting rid of me, Hazel."

No. I guess I'm not.

* * *

I slump against Robbie's shoulder, watching the baggage carousel. All three of these fuckers slept through the flight, but I didn't get a wink of sleep. The constant dull roar of circulating air, the wailing of toddlers, and gnawing claustrophobia left me exhausted and trembling by the time our wheels touched down.

Down on European soil. Prague, to be exact. The city of misfits and daredevils; Gothic spires and shot glasses of absinthe.

I can't wait to see it. To explore every alley. To stuff my face with mystery food from a menu I can't pronounce.

After I get some goddamn sleep. I'm swaying where I stand.

Robbie hums and tucks me firmer under his arm. I lay my head on his chest, my eyes drooping. Hopefully at least one of these guys remembers what my duffel bag looks like.

"Hazel."

I jerk upright, staggering into Robbie. Kamran smirks in front of me, my bag slung over his shoulder.

"Hello, sleeping beauty. I thought only horses slept standing up? Either way, time to make a move."

We find the rest of Jethro's workers clustered in the Arrivals lobby. There's a full spectrum of tiredness, from the bright eyed and well-rested through to the walking zombies like me. Eyeing the lumpy bags piled together, I'm relieved to see the equipment made it.

"All right you horrible lot!" Jethro claps his hands together. "Go catch your sleep, because you'll be giving the Czechs a five-star performance tonight."

The performers grumble, but it's the roadies with the worst luck. The rest of us can go and nap; the crew have a full day of work still ahead, setting up the venue.

"I'll see you later." Robbie presses a kiss to my temple, then hands me off to Kamran. He claps Jethro on the shoulder as he reaches his side, their heads ducking together as they walk away, talking logistics.

Not my problem, thank God. My only concern right now is finding a flat surface to sleep on.

"Shall we go find a bed?"

Kamran's finger runs up my side, tickling my ribs. I slap him away, leaning my weight on his shoulder.

"Only if you swear to keep your hands to yourself. I'm exhausted."

Kamran hums, smirking over my head at Aleksi.

"Alas. I can make no such promise."

I let him bundle me out to the taxi rank anyway, where Aleksi wanders off to read a city map. There will be no cramped trailers or Bedouin tents on this tour—it's hotels all the way. Three stars, baby! Living the good life.

Kamran hails a cab, our bags piled on the sidewalk, and I scan the view and take a deep breath.

The sights, sounds and smells of Prague fill my senses. The blare of car horns. The flutter of snowflakes caught on the breeze. The distant scent of a river.

World tour. With my favorite three guys.

Bring it on.

Author's Note

Fun fact: the setting for Cirque de la Lune was inspired by the summer I spent working for the circus. I was nowhere near the stage—I was one of the crew, dressed all in black and heaving spotlights around—but those few months were like a stolen peek into another world.

A subversive, wild, sensual world. A world in full technicolor.

Hazel's big performance is loosely based on a real performance I worked on. The trapeze artist wore a huge head-dress and massive turquoise wings. He—yes, he—danced like a bird of paradise, then 'washed' in an enormous bird bath, stripping off his costume and washing away his makeup.

It was really fucking sexy.

The beard didn't hurt, either.

Past Kayla's mind was obviously blown, because here I am years later, reliving that incredible night.

I hope I did it justice.

And I hope you loved reading about this world as much I loved living in it. *Both* times.

If you DID enjoy this book, I would be forever grateful if you'd consider leaving a review. It's a huge boost to new authors, and makes you officially an Excellent Person.

Now, go forth and do something wild with the rest of your day...

Let's keep in touch!

If you enjoy my work and you want to be the first to know what I'm up to, please consider signing up for my newsletter! I send bonus content, book recommendations, cover reveals, and other goodies twice a month.

Subscribers also get a free download of my *Lords of Summer* prequel: *Before the Fall.*

Here's a sneak peek…

* * *

She's here.

She's arrived in the quad.

Layla Mackenzie.

I glance up between the curtain of my dark hair, my elbows resting on my knees. It's still early September, barely the start of second year, and summer hasn't relinquished its hold. The air is warm—warm enough that the students dotted around the grass and on the benches are still in t-shirts. They kick back, legs stretched out, laughing in groups or studying solo.

It's the beginning of the year, and everything feels heavy with promise. With potential.

Layla picks her way across the grass, stepping over outstretched legs and winding between abandoned backpacks. She nods at a few of the groups; waves at a couple of solo students. They wave back, calling out her name, inviting her to join them.

Everyone loves Layla. What's not to love? The buttery sunshine dances over her, drawing deep bronze highlights out of her dark red hair.

Fuck.

No one makes an ass of me like Layla. I look at her creamy skin, her sweet, cheeky smile, and all words dry up in my throat. The only thing that hurts worse than looking at her is not looking at her, and every second in her presence is a sweet torture. And all the while that I'm here dying, she has no clue. She probably doesn't even know my name.

It doesn't matter. She's too good, too happy for me to let myself get near. I'm not built for sweet girls, nor for holding hands on the way to class. No gentle kisses in the sunshine. No: if I got my callused hands on her, she'd come away stained.

I couldn't bear that.

As if she can hear my thoughts, Layla glances in the direction of my bench, and I drop my gaze to my hands. I run a thumb over the opposite knuckle, back and forth, feigning interest in the scars flecking my skin.

It was a rough summer back home. It always is. Rough, but satisfying: endless days of back-breaking labor, sweetened by the jokes between workers, and at the end of the season, the tangible results. Our family ranch was built on sweat and blood, started from the ground up. It's bigger now, one of the most successful in the state, but the demands are bigger too.

The blood and sweat never go away; it's a yearly tithe, and we pay it.

I risk a glance at Layla again, to see which lucky bastards she decided to sit with, but she's gone from the center of the quad. My head jerks up fully, and I whip my gaze around, only to find her sat a few feet away on the next bench over.

My heart speeds in my chest, hammering against my rib cage, and my mouth goes dry.

Fuck. This is the problem: this is what she does to me.

She makes me foolish, reckless. Raw.

Layla sees me looking around like I've lost my puppy, because of course she does - she's not blind. I lose sight of her for fifteen seconds and the panic practically bleeds from my pores. She's not the only one who notices either; the nearest group lazing on the grass are watching me curiously too.

I let my eyes meet hers for a split second, then slide my gaze away, like I'm still looking. Like I haven't found who I'm searching for.

I swear she deflates just a little.

Fuck. I want to go over there, to just snatch up my stuff and march over to sit beside her. I want to snuff out any doubt in her mind that she's the one I'm looking for—she's always the one.

Every day, I come to the quad during lunch for the sole purpose of seeing her. I sit on this bench, or lay out on the grass—that part isn't important. What's important is that she always comes too, usually alone. And she always seems to pick out a spot near me to sit.

I don't kid myself that she does it on purpose. We've barely said ten words to each other, even since Eli started bringing her to hang out with our group. But maybe—subconsciously—she's as drawn to me as I am to her. Maybe she feels the same pull, the same fishing hook in her gut tugging her towards me.

The only relief is when she's near. Then I can breathe again.

God, I sound fucking insane.

See, this is why I can't bother the girl. If I say any of this shit out loud, if I tell her how she makes me feel, I'll be locked away in a padded room and they'll be right to do it.

Better to enjoy these stolen moments with her, then force myself back to my day.

It's not like I can tell the others, either. Eli, Jasper and Nate. I've seen the way they look at her too. We're all as fucking bad as each other.

Jealousy curls through me, hot and vicious, whenever any of my friends talk to her. And though they've never acknowledged it, they seek her out almost as much as I do. At least once a week, I'll see Jasper stood behind her in line at the campus coffee shop, leaning down with a smile curling his lips to murmur in her ear. His wavy blond hair slides forward, tickling at her cheek.

I see the shiver that runs up her spine, too. It makes me want to tear him away from her, to throw him through the huge glass window.

But when he catches up with me a few minutes later, coffee in hand, I always force a smile. What am I going to say, anyway? Hey, man, that's my dream woman that I never plan to speak to?

Nate and Eli are just as bad. Nate gets this feral glint in his eye whenever she's near, like he's putting out pheromones or some shit. A lot of girls are scared of Nate, with his buzzed head and the tattoos all over his arms and chest. But he makes Layla laugh with his savage words, the sound ringing bright between the pale stone buildings.

I long for the sound of her laugh even as I hate that I'm not the one to draw it from her.

Eli is the worst of all. He spoke to her first, got to know her in some tutorial group, so he thinks he has some kind of claim on her. It makes me want to fucking scream when he tucks an arm around her shoulders, possessive and sure.

I saw her first. I fucking craved her first.

I just never did anything about it.

Eli and Jasper round the corner to the quad, moving with confident strides. They laugh and talk as they walk, raising a hand each when they notice me. We found each other during orientation week of first year, Nate included. It was so fucking easy, like four jigsaw pieces slotting into place.

I've never had that before. Not with friends, and certainly not with family. What we have, the four of us—it's like breathing. Unconscious and vital.

Both of their eyes light up when they notice Layla on the next bench over. I have to remind myself then that these guys are brothers to me —that I can't lose my shit over a dumb surge of jealousy.

Then Eli strides straight past my bench to sit next to Layla. A dark curl falls over his forehead, and his eyes crinkle when he speaks.

No. No, he can't tuck her hair behind her ear—can't make her blush like that. I shoot a glance at Jasper to see what he thinks, but he's watching the two of them with heat in his gaze. I want to shake him, then rip Eli away from Layla and shake him too. Can't they see how wrong this is?

It should be me on that fucking bench.

I tried to stay away for so long. Since the first time I saw Layla, way back in October of first year. I thought I could protect us both by keeping away, but now she's everywhere I look, and my friends have set their sights on her.

Fuck that. I won't bow out without a fight.

Today is the day I tell Layla Mackenzie how I feel.

Teaser: Knights of Winter

We were only supposed to be here for two weeks, but the snowstorm traps us in the castle together.

Asher: the sweet, noble guy who wants me all to himself.

Lance: his grumpy best friend who can't seem to keep away.

Morgan: the tutor I should NOT be crushing on.

And me, Freaky Gigi. The girl who finds normal conversations to be minefields.

But we're not alone in the Welsh mountains. And soon, we're not safe.

It's time to show everyone how badass Freaky Gigi can be.

Knights of Winter is a standalone contemporary reverse harem novel. It contains explicit language, high heat, and a guaranteed HEA.

Available now on Amazon.

Read on for a sneak preview…

* * *

The wind billows into my hood and tears it back from my head. Icy sleet hammers my cheeks and eyes, droplets clinging to my glasses and making me half-blind. I yank my hood back up and hold it there, rain sliding down my wrist into my sleeve as I hurry across campus.

The clouds hang low overhead, dark gray and swollen, and street lamps glow orange even though it's barely 4pm. Laughter breaks out across the quad and I flinch, ducking my head.

I'm not a coward. But I'm too busy to stand up for myself right now. I have a list to check; plans to make; dreams to make real.

Those frat boys will have to entertain themselves for today. I angle myself away from them as I cross the paved courtyard, smiling in the depths of my hood.

I've waited months for this afternoon.

The automatic glass door to the History building shudders to the side as I approach. It's a cruel irony: the History department is housed in the most modern building on campus, a monstrosity of glass and steel. It's all straight lines and sharp edges; no mystery, no heart.

I mentioned it to one of the professors once, and he blinked around the lecture hall like he'd never seen it before.

The Mathematics department, meanwhile, is in a listed colonial brownstone. Go figure.

Warm, stale air washes over me as I squelch into the lobby. I let my hood drop, shaking out my head and arms like a dog. Raindrops shower onto the glossy black tiles, and steam creeps around the edge of my glasses.

Another laugh breaks out somewhere down the nearest corridor and I jerk, heart thumping. Flattening a palm on my chest, I will my racing heart to calm down as I drift out of the lobby towards Professor Walsh's office. It's late afternoon in the history department, not midnight in a graveyard.

Besides, there's nothing these assholes can say to me that they haven't said before. Sticks and stones, and all that. I gust out a long breath and wander down the long corridor.

There. I walked a mile in the rain to see this: a sheet of A4 paper tacked to Professor Walsh's office door, ink smudged and corners curling. He could have sent an email, of course, but that's not Walsh's style. Tradition over convenience, never mind the icy December rain.

I may be a history nerd, but at least I've embraced modern technology.

The paper taunts me from half the corridor away, a pale, blurry rectangle against the wood of the door. I pull my glasses off as I approach, wiping them with the cloth I keep tucked in my pocket, then sliding them back on my nose.

It's a short list. Only six names, even though over eighty students applied.

And who wouldn't? A funded trip to a legendary castle, half the world away? The chance to page through books in ancient libraries and sleep in the same rooms where historical figures once slept?

I scan the list, my heart leaping into my throat at the fifth name.

Gigi Russell.

"Yes!" I hiss, pumping the air. "Hell yes."

"Steady on, Gigi," a voice drawls behind my shoulder. "You're practically cursing."

Just like that, my soaring mood falters. I purse my lips and turn around.

Lance Lockford smirks down at me, his tawny hair slick with rain. It slides down his temples, down the pale column of his throat, and disappears into the neckline of his sweatshirt.

"My eyes are up here, you know."

I jerk my gaze back up to his, heat prickling over my cheeks. He always does this, always makes me tongue-tied and stupid. Teasing me is one of Lance Lockford's favorite games.

"What do you want, Lockford?"

Lance rolls his eyes and steps forward, crowding me back against the office door. He lifts one hand, and for a ridiculous moment, I think he's going to stroke my cheek or play with my hair. He does that sometimes. Pets a stray curl, or chucks me under the chin. I hate those moments and yearn for them in equal measure.

My mouth drops open, and I blink up at him with my chest heaving beneath the sodden bundle of my scarf. With his hair wet, I can smell the faint scent of his shampoo.

Lance reaches past me and taps a finger against the sheet of paper. He traces the list, his finger dragging over the names.

"Perfect." He smirks at my flushed cheeks as I glower up at him, disappointed. "All my favorite people on one trip."

No. I whirl around, my elbow catching him in the side. He grunts and steps back as I read the list again.

I'd been so focused on finding my own name, I hadn't properly read the others.

Lance Lockford, Asher Penderly and his sister Melissa.

The three people I try most to avoid.

Not because they're cruel, like the frat boys, but because the sight of the three of them together leaves me hollow. They're so comfortable. So intimate. All inside jokes and casual touches.

I don't remember the last physical contact I had that wasn't a handshake.

Plus there's Lance's teasing, and Asher's kind smiles that crinkle his eyes at the corners…

"You can't," I mumble, lips numb.

"Can't what?" Lance snaps, annoyed now. "Can't go on a college trip because Freaky Gigi says so?"

I breathe hard, fogging up my own glasses, and step to one side, shaking my head. I don't look at Lance. I don't have my features under control.

"You don't even like this class." I sound strangled. "None of you do. You missed half the lectures."

"Keeping tabs on us, were you?"

I swallow and jerk my head again, even though the answer is yes. Whenever they're near, I can't tear my eyes away. And whenever they're gone, I feel a soothing, dull relief.

This can't be happening. I can't win a place on the trip of a lifetime, then ruin it before we've even gone.

I turn to Lance, eyes pleading.

"We were supposed to be chosen based on grades."

The last dregs of humor drain from his face, leaving him colder than the December sleet. When Lance speaks, he spits each word at me.

"Just because we're not weird and friendless doesn't mean we're fucking stupid."

I flinch. It's so much worse coming from him. Lance is moodier than the other two, yes, with a frown that settles over his brow when he thinks no one is looking. But as soon as there are people around, he's all cocky smiles and teasing jokes. I always try to sit out of his eye line but within earshot, so I can hear the steady stream of his one liners.

The class entertainer.

He's not laughing now.

"That's not what I meant," I whisper, but it's too late. Lance turns on his heel and strides away.

I know the trio are all smart. But really, all three of them winning a place? After their attendance was so poor?

It's statistically highly unlikely. That's all I meant to say.

I turn back to read the list a final time, chewing on my bottom lip. This, right here, is why I'm better off alone. Even when I like someone, even when I mean well, I screw it all up. It's like everyone else got a secret script when they were growing up—a How To for social interaction.

I close my eyes and thump my forehead against the door.

Freaky Gigi strikes again.

About the Author

Kayla Wren is a British author who writes steamy New Adult romance. She loves Reverse Harem, Enemies-to-Lovers, and Forbidden Love tropes.

Kayla writes prickly men with hearts of gold, secretly-sexy geeks, and—best of all—she's ALWAYS had a thing for the villains.

You can connect with me on:
🌐 https://www.kaylawrenauthor.com
📘 https://www.facebook.com/kaylawrenauthor
🔗 https://www.bookbub.com/authors/kayla-wren

Subscribe to my newsletter:
✉️ https://newsletter.kaylawrenauthor.com/beforethefall

Also by Kayla Wren

Lords of Summer
They tortured me all year at college.

Now I'm working the summer as their maid.

Lords of Summer is the first installment in the Year of the Harem collection.

Available now on Amazon.